Head to Toe

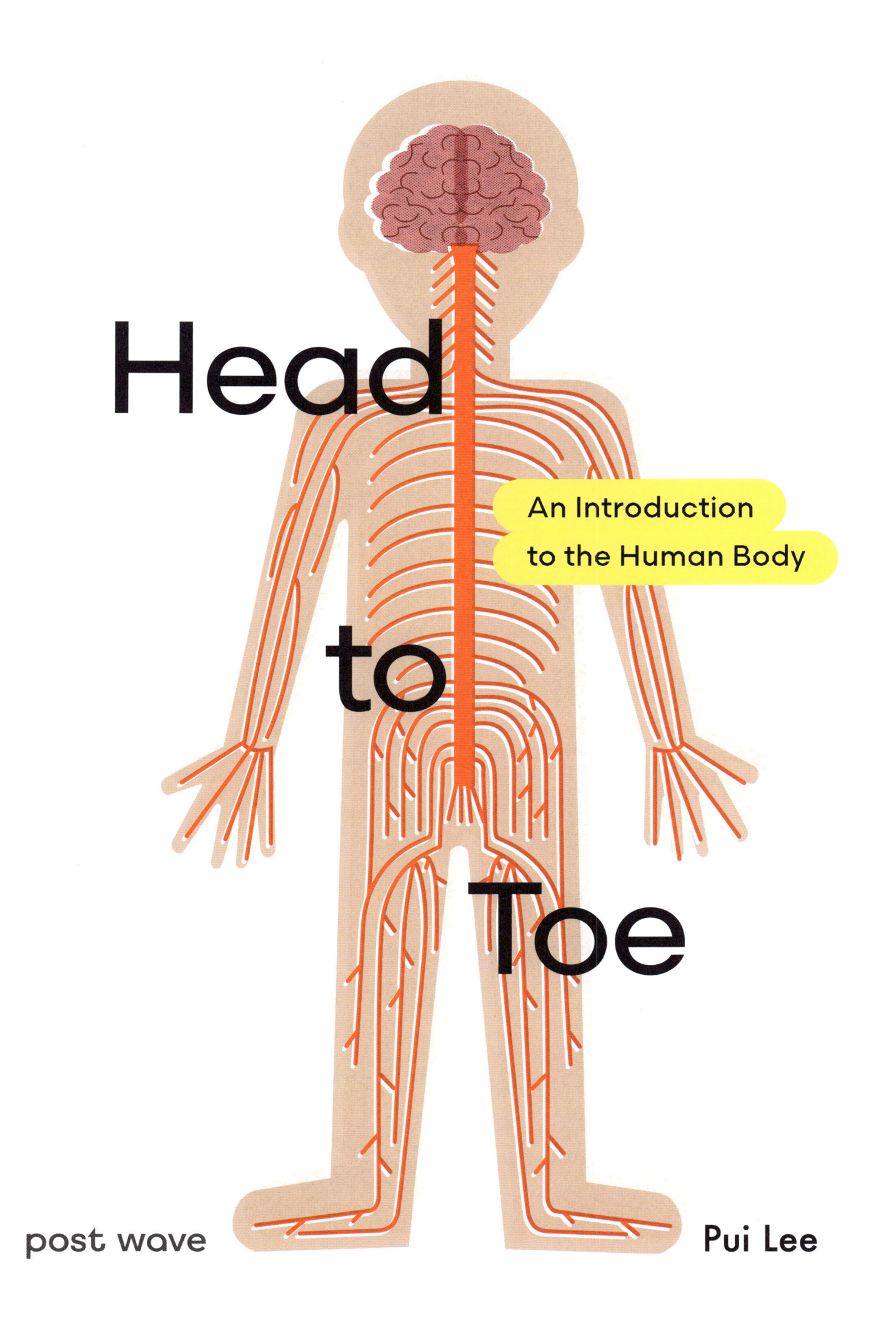

Head to Toe

An Introduction to the Human Body

post wave

Pui Lee

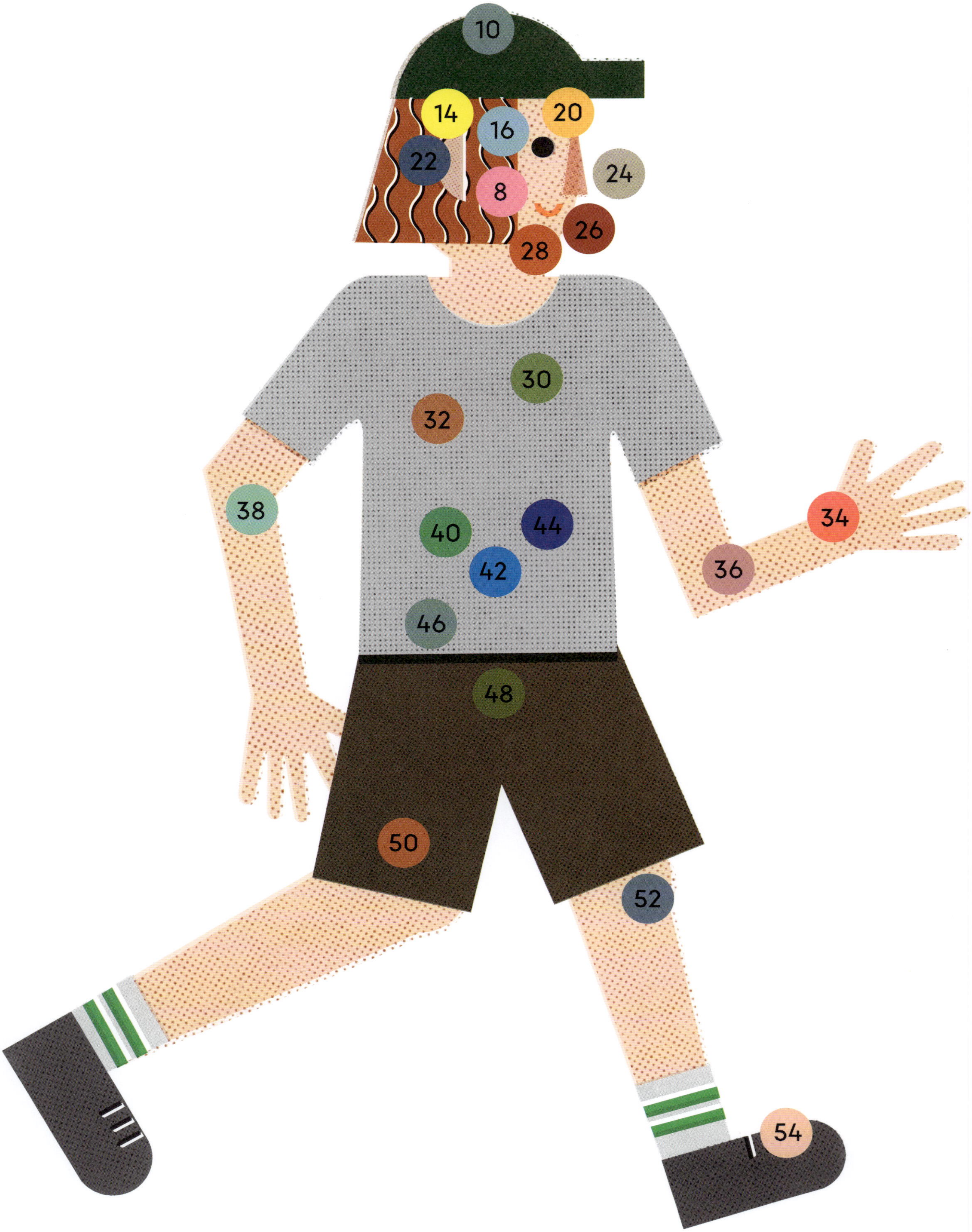
10
14
20
16
22
24
8
26
28
30
32
38
34
40
44
36
42
46
48
50
52
54

Contents

6		Welcome to Your Body!
8	●	Face Shapes
10	●	Brain
14	●	Hair
16	●	Eyes
20	●	Eyelashes and Eyebrows
22	●	Ears
24	●	Nose
26	●	Mouth and Teeth
28	●	Tongue
30	●	Heart
32	●	Lungs
34	●	Hands
36	●	Skin
38	●	Blood
40	●	Kidneys
42	●	Stomach
44	●	Liver and Pancreas
46	●	Intestines
48	●	Cells and Reproduction
50	●	Muscles and Tendons
52	●	Bones and Joints
54	●	Feet
56		Head to Toe
58		Body Facts
60		Glossary
62		Further Reading and References
63		About the Author

Welcome to Your Body!

Have you ever wondered what makes your heart beat, how many memories your brain can store or why your eyes are a different colour from somebody else's? We are going to delve inside and out of the human body to discover what makes us tick. From organs and tissues, to what makes us all different on the outside, we will explore all these questions and much more.

The human body is special and comes in all shapes and sizes, making each one of us unique. So, let's get ready to explore and celebrate our bodies – from head to toe!

OVAL

An oval-shaped face is longer than it is wide, with its features evenly spaced out.

RECTANGLE

A rectangular face is longer than it is wide, with a square jaw and a high forehead.

Face Shapes

No single person on the planet has the same face – not even identical twins! The shape of our face is a big part of what makes us unique and recognisable. Faces can be round, oval, square, heart-shaped – or even a mix of shapes! The shape affects how our features (like our eyes, nose and mouth) look. This is what makes each of us one of a kind.

Which face shape do you have?

ROUND

A round face shape is characterised by a wide hairline and full cheeks.

SQUARE

A square face has a strong jawline, a wide hairline and a shape that is roughly the same width and length.

DIAMOND

This is the rarest face shape. It is defined by a narrow hairline, wide cheekbones and a pointed chin.

HEART

A heart-shaped face has a wide forehead, high cheekbones and a narrow chin.

9

Brain

The brain is a very complex **organ** responsible for most of our bodies' functions. It controls everything we do! It has the ability to send and receive lots of information – the human body sends an enormous amount to the brain every second! However, the conscious mind (the part of the brain that is aware of what you're doing right now) can only focus on a tiny fraction of it. This means our brains handle huge amounts of information without us even knowing.

Size Doesn't Matter

The human brain continues to develop until around your forties, after which it starts to shrink a bit. But don't worry! There is no evidence that a larger brain is smarter than a smaller one. What really matters is how well your brain works. So, it's important to keep your brain active and healthy.

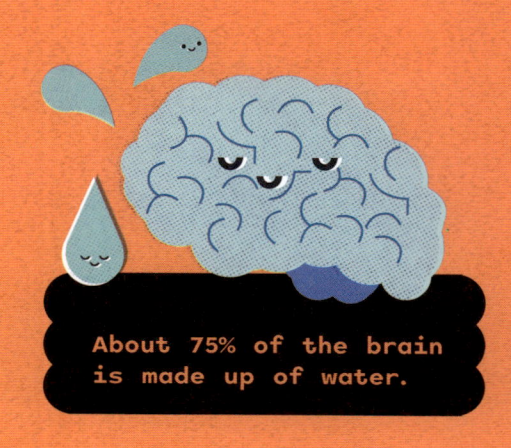

About 75% of the brain is made up of water.

Automatic Breathing

The brain manages your breathing when you're awake and asleep. The **brainstem** (the lower part of the brain) monitors the amount of **oxygen** and **carbon dioxide** in your body, and sends signals to your muscles to breathe in or out more. This happens all the time, without you thinking about it.

Brain vs. Supercomputer

The human brain is amazing at recognising faces. It can spot a familiar face in just a fraction of a second, even if the person looks different or hasn't been seen in years. Supercomputers need lots of data and time to do the same thing, and they still aren't as good at it as our brains!

Left Brain and Right Brain

There's a popular idea that people are either 'left-brained' or 'right-brained' thinkers. The left side of the brain is often linked to logic, language and problem-solving, while the right side is thought to handle creativity, emotions and imagination. In reality, both sides of the brain work together for almost everything we do. For example, when solving puzzles or making music, different parts of the brain team up and work together. So, while some people might be better at certain skills, we all use our whole brain in different ways!

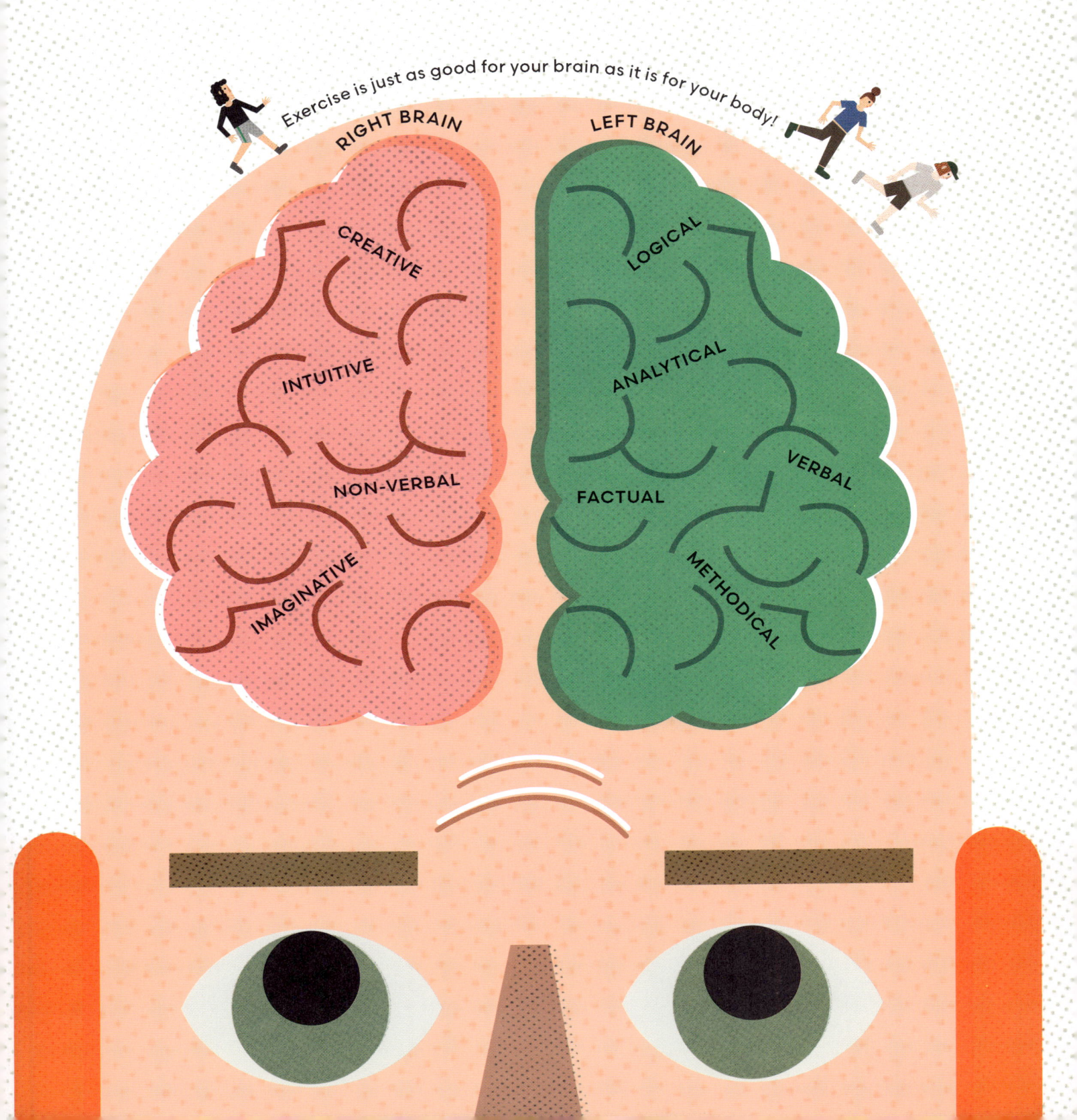

Exercise is just as good for your brain as it is for your body!

RIGHT BRAIN
- CREATIVE
- INTUITIVE
- NON-VERBAL
- IMAGINATIVE

LEFT BRAIN
- LOGICAL
- ANALYTICAL
- FACTUAL
- VERBAL
- METHODICAL

Brain Power

It's important to keep our brains healthy. Good mental health affects how we think, feel and do things. When our mental health is good, our brain can focus better, remember things and help us enjoy life more. But if someone is struggling with their mental health, their brain might find it hard to concentrate or feel happy. We can take care of our brains by getting plenty of rest, eating healthy food and doing things we enjoy.

Memory
When the brain creates a new memory or learns something new, it stores the memory in the tiny gaps between brain cells called **synapses**. It also forms new connections between these cells, helping to reshape and strengthen the brain.

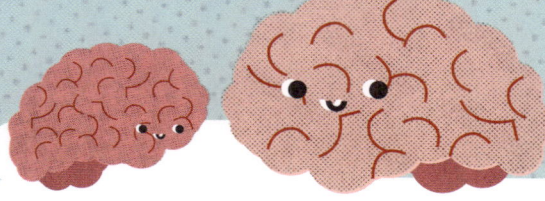

Short- and Long-Term Memory
Our brain has two different types of memory. Short-term memory lasts about 20-30 seconds and is a bit like a notepad for jotting things down quickly. But our long-term memory is like a library, capable of storing a lifetime of memories.

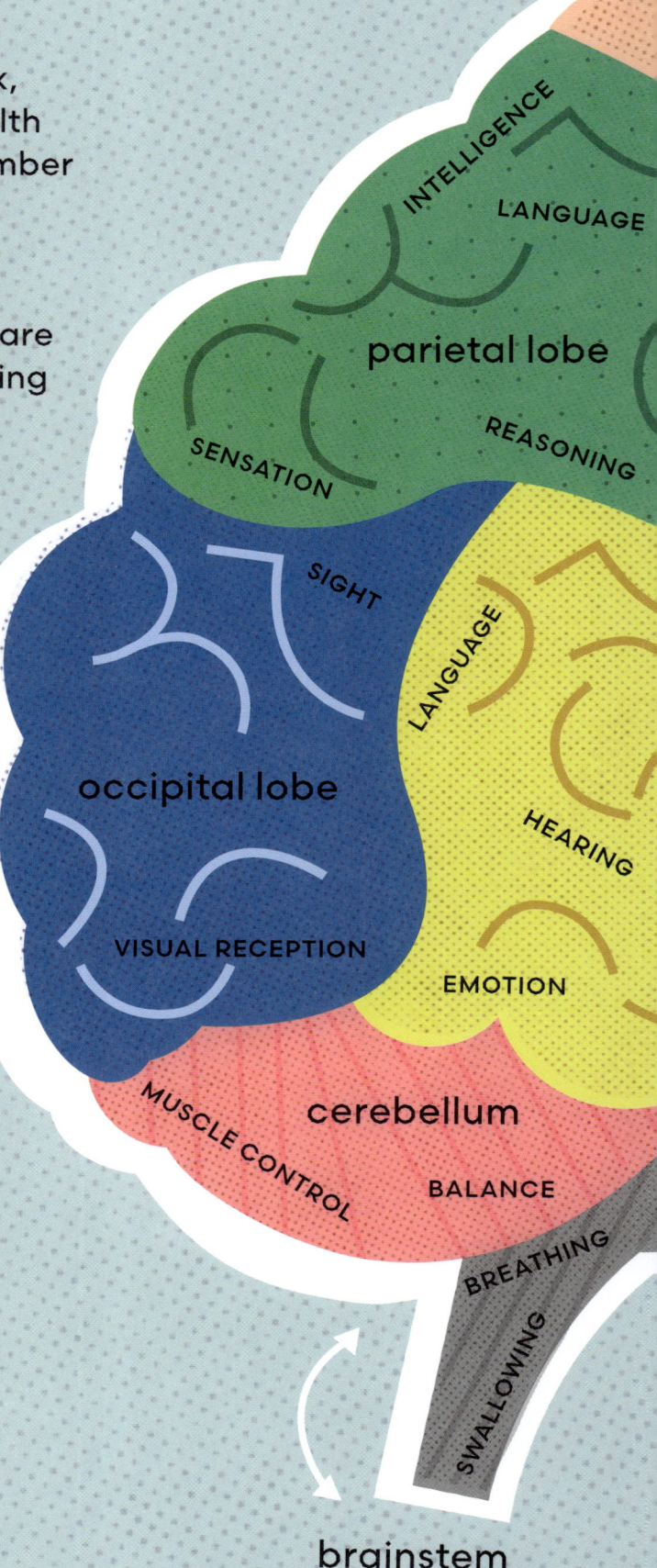

INTELLIGENCE
LANGUAGE
parietal lobe
REASONING
SENSATION
SIGHT
LANGUAGE
occipital lobe
HEARING
VISUAL RECEPTION
EMOTION
MUSCLE CONTROL
cerebellum
BALANCE
BREATHING
SWALLOWING
brainstem

MOVEMENT SPEECH

frontal lobe

PROBLEM SOLVING

BEHAVIOUR

temporal lobe

MEMORY

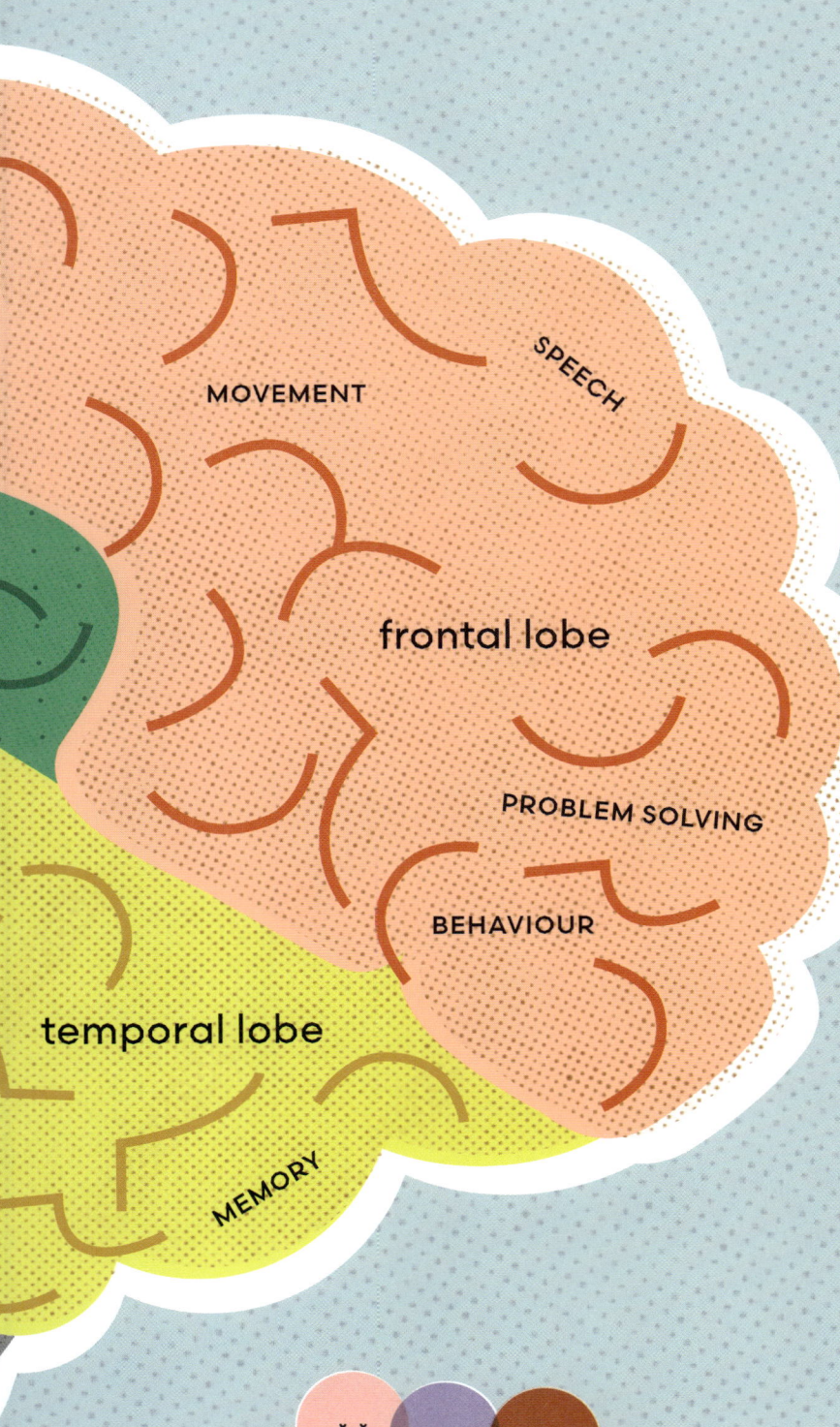

Circadian Rhythm

This is the body's internal clock. It helps control what we do in a 24-hour cycle, like being awake during the day and asleep at night. It also affects things like hunger, digestion, body temperature and **hormones**.

Sleep

Sleep is important for your body and brain to work well. Without enough sleep, your brain can't work at its best. While you sleep, your brain collects all the memories from the day. Scientists think we dream to process emotions, solve problems and understand what we've learned. Most people have between four and seven dreams a night, but you might not remember them all.

Emotions

Emotions are the way our brain gives meaning to feelings, based on our past experiences. Different networks in the brain work together to create feelings such as happiness, surprise, sadness and anger.

Daydreaming

A wandering mind happens when your brain takes a break from focussing on tasks. This allows your thoughts to flow freely from one idea to another, sometimes leading to more creative thinking.

Beards

Beards are among the fastest-growing hairs on the body! Teenagers usually start growing them because of changes to their hormones (chemicals in the body). How fast beards and other facial hair grows can also depend on **genetics**, seasons and diet.

Unique Hair

Black hair is the most common natural hair colour in the world, while red hair is the rarest. People from different **ethnicities** have different hair types.

Some have curly hair, some have straight hair and others have wavy hair. But all hair types are beautiful!

Hair

As well as being fun to style, your hair is very important! It helps protect your head from the sun and keeps you warm when it is cold. You actually have hairs all over your body – some are long, like the hair on your head, but some are very short and fine, such as the tiny hairs in our nose and ears. The hairs on our arms and legs are also very sensitive and can detect changes in temperature.

Hair is a fun way to express your character. It can be cut, dyed, braided or styled in many different ways to show who you are and what you like.

Albinism

Some people have very light skin, hair and eyes because they have a condition called albinism. This happens when their body makes less melanin, the pigment that gives colour. Albinism can affect anyone but it is quite rare – about one in 20,000 people have it.

How Fast Does Hair Grow?

Hair grows about 15cm a year, or 1.25cm a month. Sometimes, people lose their hair as they get older, or because of their genes or a condition called male- or female-pattern baldness.

Eyes

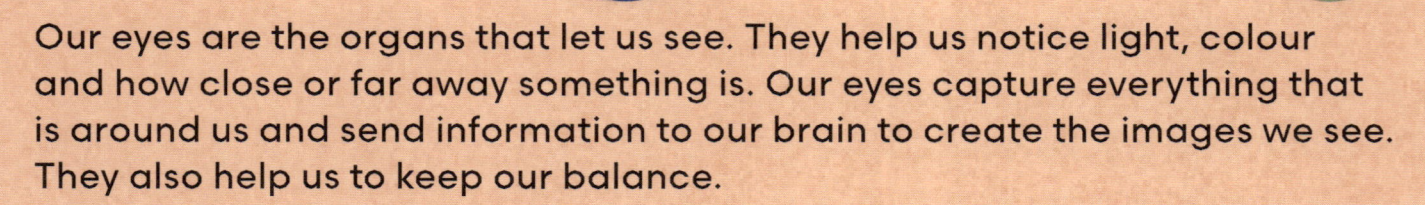

Our eyes are the organs that let us see. They help us notice light, colour and how close or far away something is. Our eyes capture everything that is around us and send information to our brain to create the images we see. They also help us to keep our balance.

Colour Vision

The human eye can detect around 10 million different colours! We have special cells in our eyes called cones that let us see different colours. There are three types of cones: one for red, one for green and one for blue.

Eyes can come in many different colours, from blue to green to hazel. Brown is the most common eye colour in the world. Your eye colour depends on your **DNA** and the genetics of your parents. The pigment melanin gives colour to your eyes – more melanin means darker eyes, while less melanin results in lighter eyes.

`Your eyes can process 36,000 pieces of information in a single hour!`

`'Heterochromia' is the term for different coloured eyes in the same person.`

Vision

Our eyes are crucial for seeing and understanding the world, so it is important to take good care of them. There are lots of ways we can keep our vision strong and our eyes healthy.

Glasses

Some people need glasses to see better. If they are short-sighted, they can see things up close but not far away. If they are long-sighted, they can see far away but not up close. Glasses make everything clear and sharp. Sunglasses also protect our eyes from bright light and harmful rays.

Take a Break

When we watch TV or look at a computer screen, it's important to rest our eyes afterwards to prevent strain. Eye strain happens when our eyes get tired from focussing for too long.

Eating With Your Eyes

Vitamin A is essential for good eyesight. It can be found in foods like carrots, asparagus, apricots and nectarines.

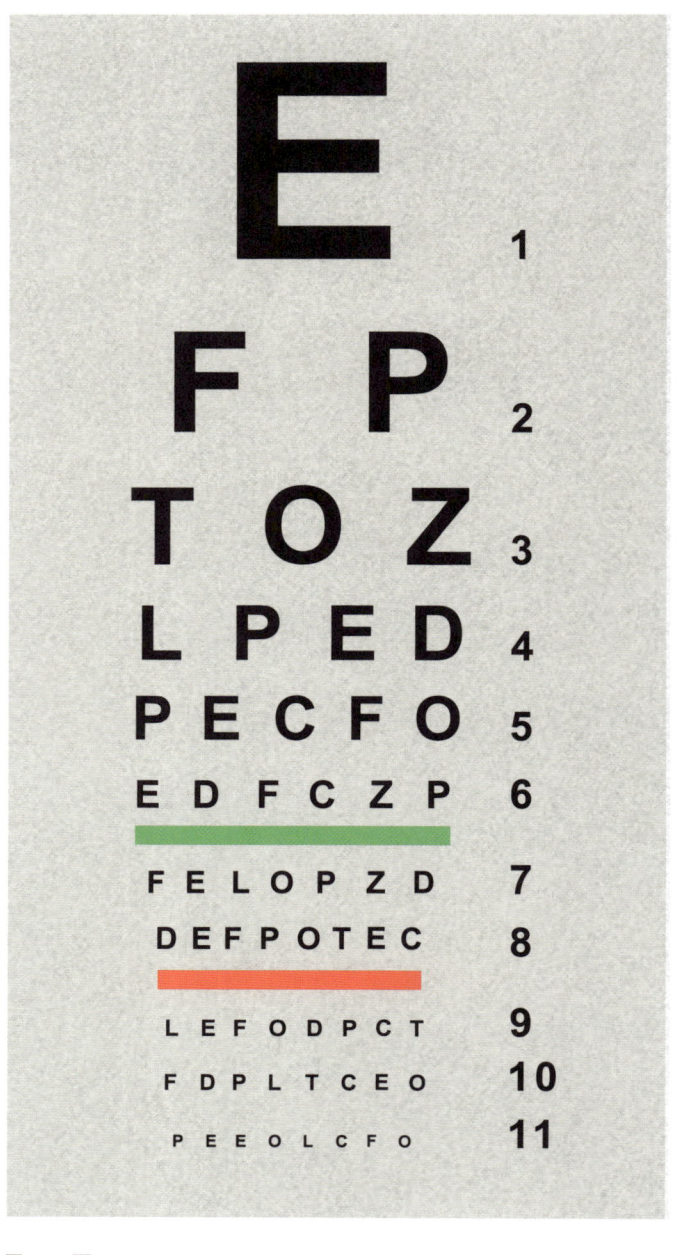

E	1
F P	2
T O Z	3
L P E D	4
P E C F O	5
E D F C Z P	6
F E L O P Z D	7
D E F P O T E C	8
L E F O D P C T	9
F D P L T C E O	10
P E E O L C F O	11

Eye Tests

It's recommended to have an eye test every two years or as your optician suggests. An eye test checks how well you see straight ahead and your side (peripheral) vision. Regular eye tests can identify vision problems early on.

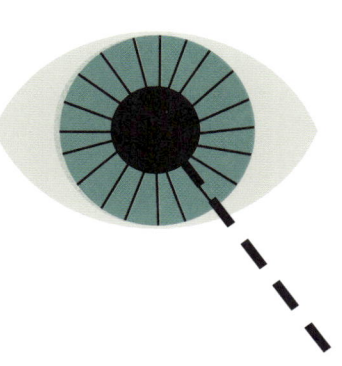

20/20 Vision

20/20 vision refers to a person who can clearly read an eye chart when they are standing 20 feet (6 metres) away. It is a term used to describe normal eyesight.

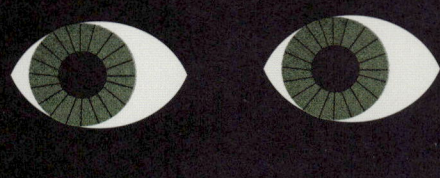

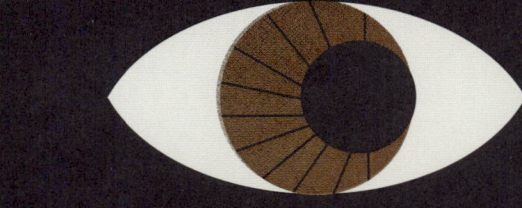

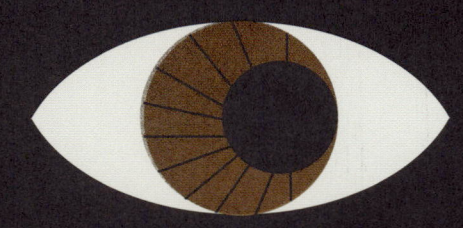

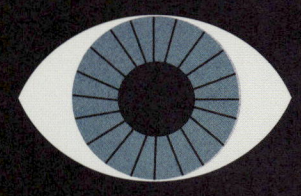

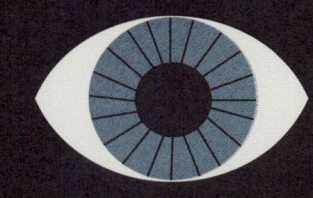

Humans can see in the dark, but it takes time for our eyes to adjust. It can take anywhere from a few seconds to a minute for our pupils to expand and let more light in.

How Do Eyes Work?

Our eyes work a bit like a camera. Light enters through a clear part called the cornea and then passes through the pupil, which is the black circle in the middle. The light then hits the lens, which focuses it onto the retina at the back of the eye. The retina changes the light into signals that travel to the brain, which then tells us what we are seeing.

Anatomy of the Eye

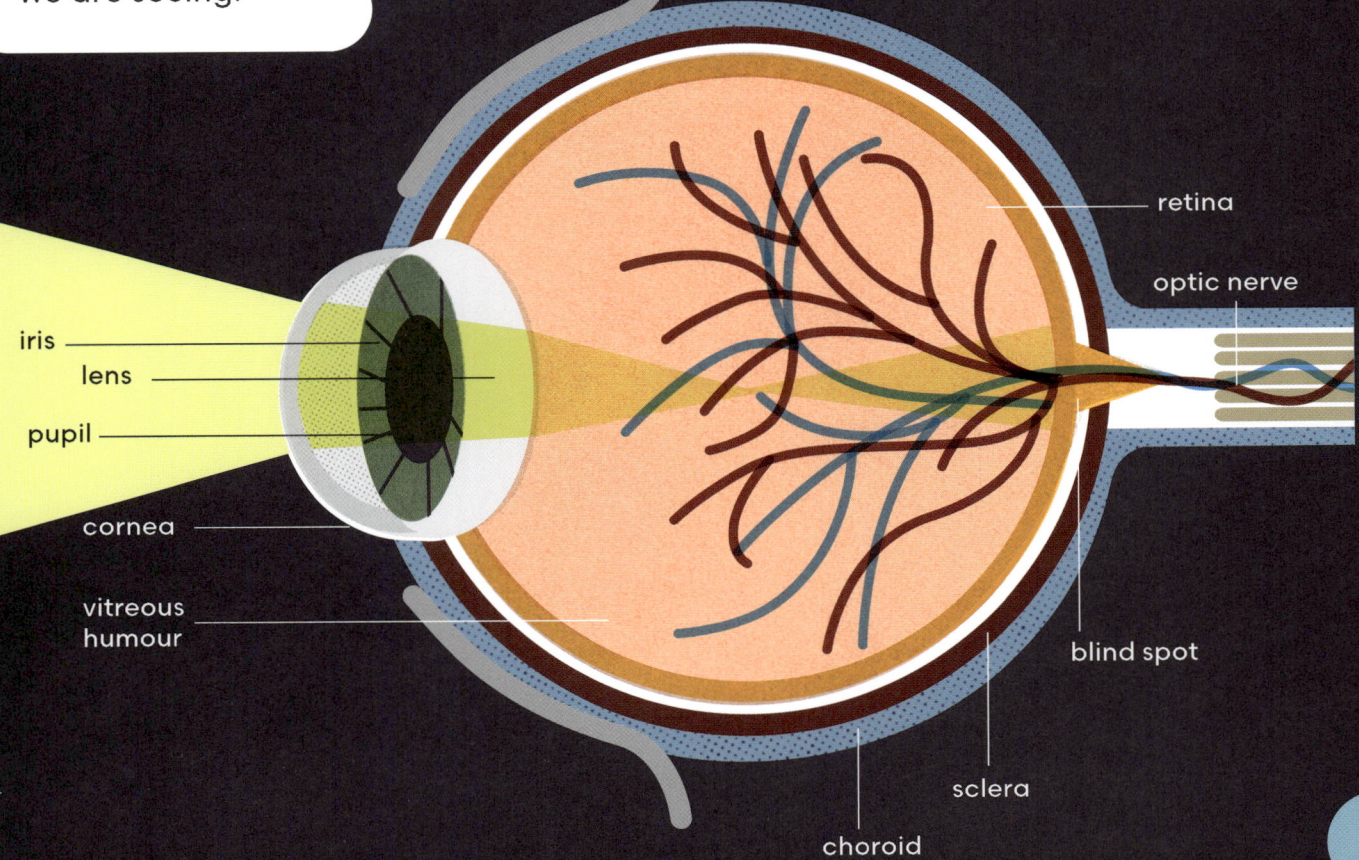

- iris
- lens
- pupil
- cornea
- vitreous humour
- retina
- optic nerve
- blind spot
- sclera
- choroid

19

> We lose up to 5 eyelashes a day, and it takes each eyelash between 1 and 3 months to grow back.

We blink more than 20,000 times a day or almost eight million times a year! Each blink cleans our eyes.

Eyelashes and Eyebrows

Eyebrows and eyelashes help protect our eyes by keeping out dust, dirt, light and sweat. Eyelashes catch particles before they enter our eyes, while eyebrows prevent sweat and rain from running into them. They also frame our face and express our emotions. Interestingly, it's quite tricky to recognise someone without their eyebrows!

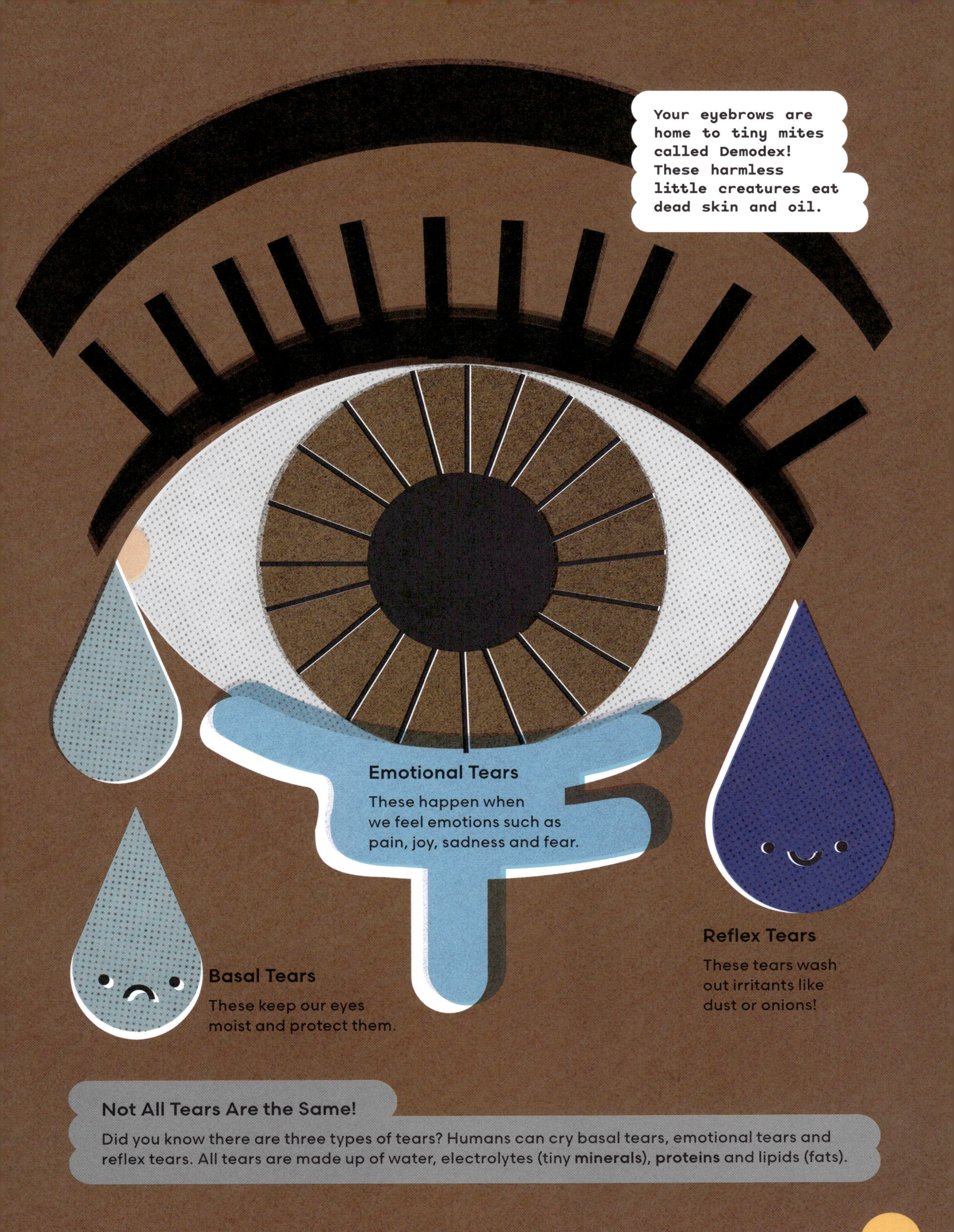

> Your eyebrows are home to tiny mites called Demodex! These harmless little creatures eat dead skin and oil.

Emotional Tears
These happen when we feel emotions such as pain, joy, sadness and fear.

Basal Tears
These keep our eyes moist and protect them.

Reflex Tears
These tears wash out irritants like dust or onions!

Not All Tears Are the Same!
Did you know there are three types of tears? Humans can cry basal tears, emotional tears and reflex tears. All tears are made up of water, electrolytes (tiny **minerals**), **proteins** and lipids (fats).

Ears

Our ears are amazing parts of our body that do important work. They help us hear and keep us balanced. We have two ears so our brain can receive sound from both sides, which helps us figure out where sounds are coming from. Having two ears also helps us understand space and volume, so we can hear better.

1

OUTER EAR

Ears are self-cleaning! Earwax is anti-fungal and antibacterial, helping to prevent dirt from entering the ear.

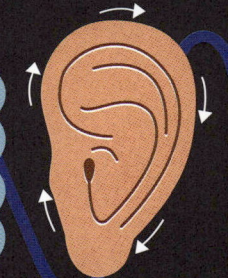

How Loud is That Sound?

Sound is measured in decibels. Humans can hear sounds starting from around 0 decibels (dB), which is the quietest level the human ear can detect, to 140 dB, which can be as loud as a rock concert. Sounds above 80 dB can damage our hearing, and sounds above 130 dB can cause pain.

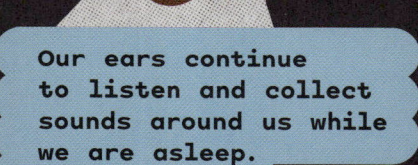

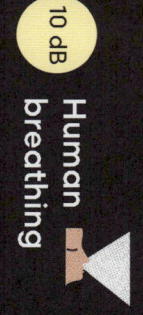

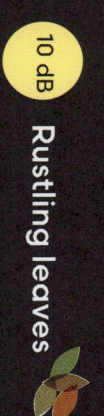

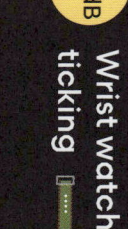

Our ears continue to listen and collect sounds around us while we are asleep.

- 10 dB — Human breathing
- 10 dB — Rustling leaves
- 20 dB — Wrist watch ticking
- 40 dB — Quiet library
- 50 dB — Light rain
- 60 dB — Background music
- 70 dB — Dog barking
- 75 dB — Ice cream van
- 80 dB — Alarm clock

Anatomy of the Ear

Key
1. Outer ear (pinna)
2. Ear canal
3. Eardrum
4. Ossicles
5. Cochlea
6. Auditory nerve
7. Vestibular nerve
8. Semicircular canals
9. Mastoid bone

MIDDLE EAR

Our ears constantly get bigger as we get older. They never stop!

85 dB City traffic
90 dB Hairdryer
95 dB Motorcycle
120 dB Fireworks

How Do Ears Work?

The outer ear collects **sound waves** and sends them through the ear canal to the eardrum, which vibrates when the sound waves hit it. These vibrations pass through the **ossicles** (three tiny bones called the hammer, anvil and stirrup) which make the sound stronger.

Next, the vibrations reach the cochlea in the inner ear, where they are turned into electrical signals. These signals travel through the auditory nerve to the brain, where they are processed so we can understand sounds.

The vestibular nerve and semicircular canals help us stay balanced, while the mastoid bone protects parts of the ear and helps with hearing.

Nose

The nose is part of the **respiratory system** that helps you breathe and smell. It filters the air and cleans it before you breathe it in. Inside your nose are tiny hairs and mucus that trap dirt and germs, keeping the air going into your lungs fresh and healthy.

> A single sneeze can travel up to 160km an hour — as fast as a race car!

AaAchooOO!

> Our noses can detect over one trillion different smells!

How Does the Nose Work?

The nose helps us smell by detecting tiny scent particles in the air. When you sniff, these particles travel into your nose through the nasal cavity. Inside, a special area called the olfactory epithelium has millions of tiny sensors. These sensors pick up the smell and send signals to the olfactory bulb in your brain. The brain then figures out what the smell is, like flowers or food.

Key
1. Nasal cavity
2. Olfactory epithelium
3. Olfactory nerves
4. Olfactory bulb

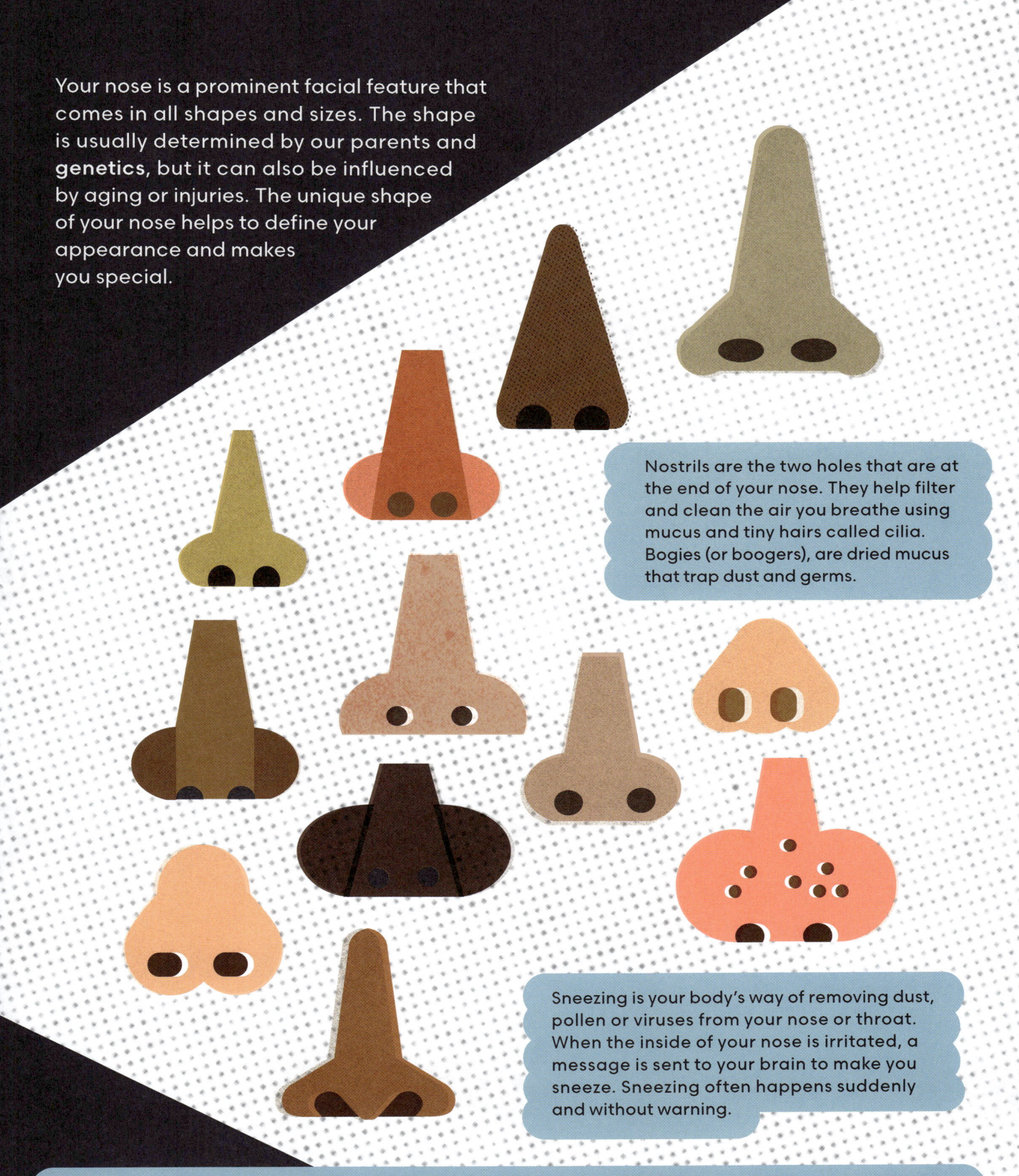

Your nose is a prominent facial feature that comes in all shapes and sizes. The shape is usually determined by our parents and **genetics**, but it can also be influenced by aging or injuries. The unique shape of your nose helps to define your appearance and makes you special.

Nostrils are the two holes that are at the end of your nose. They help filter and clean the air you breathe using mucus and tiny hairs called cilia. Bogies (or boogers), are dried mucus that trap dust and germs.

Sneezing is your body's way of removing dust, pollen or viruses from your nose or throat. When the inside of your nose is irritated, a message is sent to your brain to make you sneeze. Sneezing often happens suddenly and without warning.

Our noses can detect over one trillion different smells! Good smells, like fresh bread or flowers, can make us happy, trigger memories and tell us food is safe to eat. Bad smells, like rotten eggs or smoke, warn us of danger, or remind us to stay clean. Both good and bad smells play important roles in keeping us healthy and safe.

Mouth and Teeth

Your brilliant mouth helps you eat, talk and smile! It includes your teeth, tongue and lips, all working together.

Your teeth are as unique as your fingerprints! Their shape, size, alignment and patterns are different for every person. Most adults have 32 permanent teeth: 8 incisors, 4 canines, 8 premolars and 12 molars (including 4 wisdom teeth). Children have 20 teeth, until about age 6 when their adult teeth start to come through.

Growth Timeline

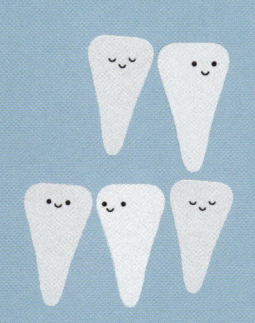

Baby Teeth
From 5 months

Also known as milk teeth, or first teeth, baby teeth become worn down from biting and chewing. As the jaw and mouth grow bigger, more, larger teeth are also needed to eat with. Baby teeth naturally fall out as you grow.

Incisors and Canines
From 6 years

Incisors are the sharp teeth at the front of the mouth. They help us grip and rip food into smaller pieces. Canines are the pointy teeth next to the incisors. They help us tear and chew food.

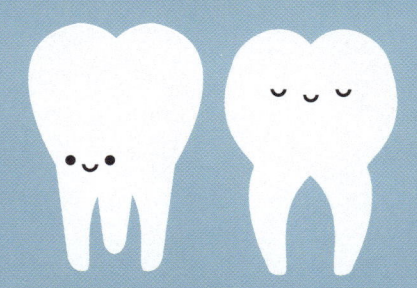

Premolars and Molars
From 9 to 13 years

Premolars are smaller teeth found in the middle of the mouth, between the front canines and the back molars. They help us grind and chew food. Molars are chunkier, located at the back of the mouth, and they help us grind, crush and chew. Baby molars come in first and are later replaced by adult molars from age 6, and premolars from age 10.

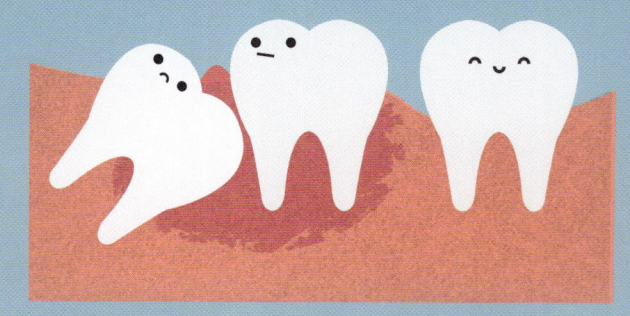

Wisdom Teeth
From 17 years

Wisdom teeth are the last set of molars to come through at the back of the mouth. These teeth were useful during the Stone Age for grinding tough raw plants and meat, but today our diets are softer, so they are no longer necessary. It's common for them to be removed to make space for other teeth.

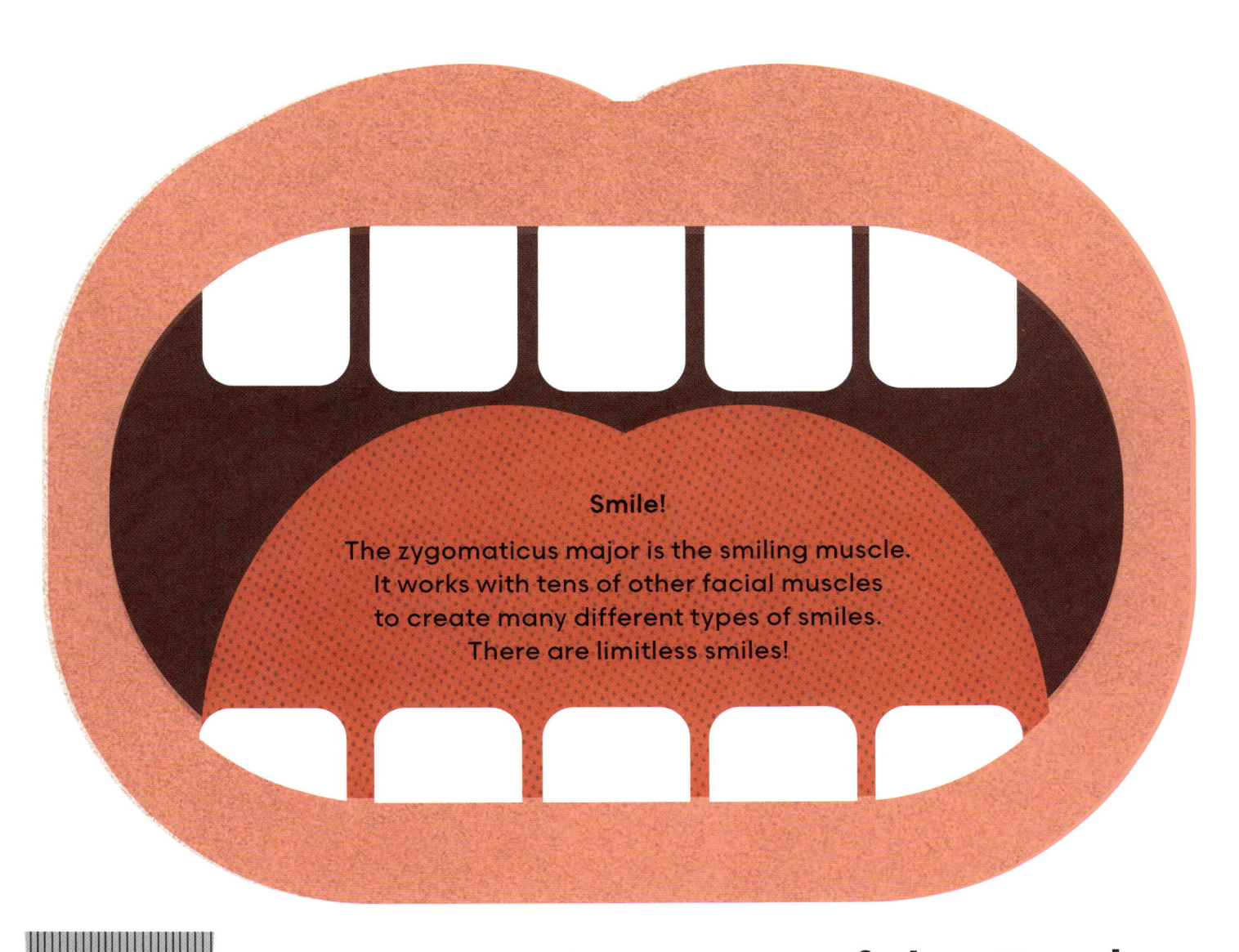

Smile!

The zygomaticus major is the smiling muscle. It works with tens of other facial muscles to create many different types of smiles. There are limitless smiles!

Anatomy of the Tooth

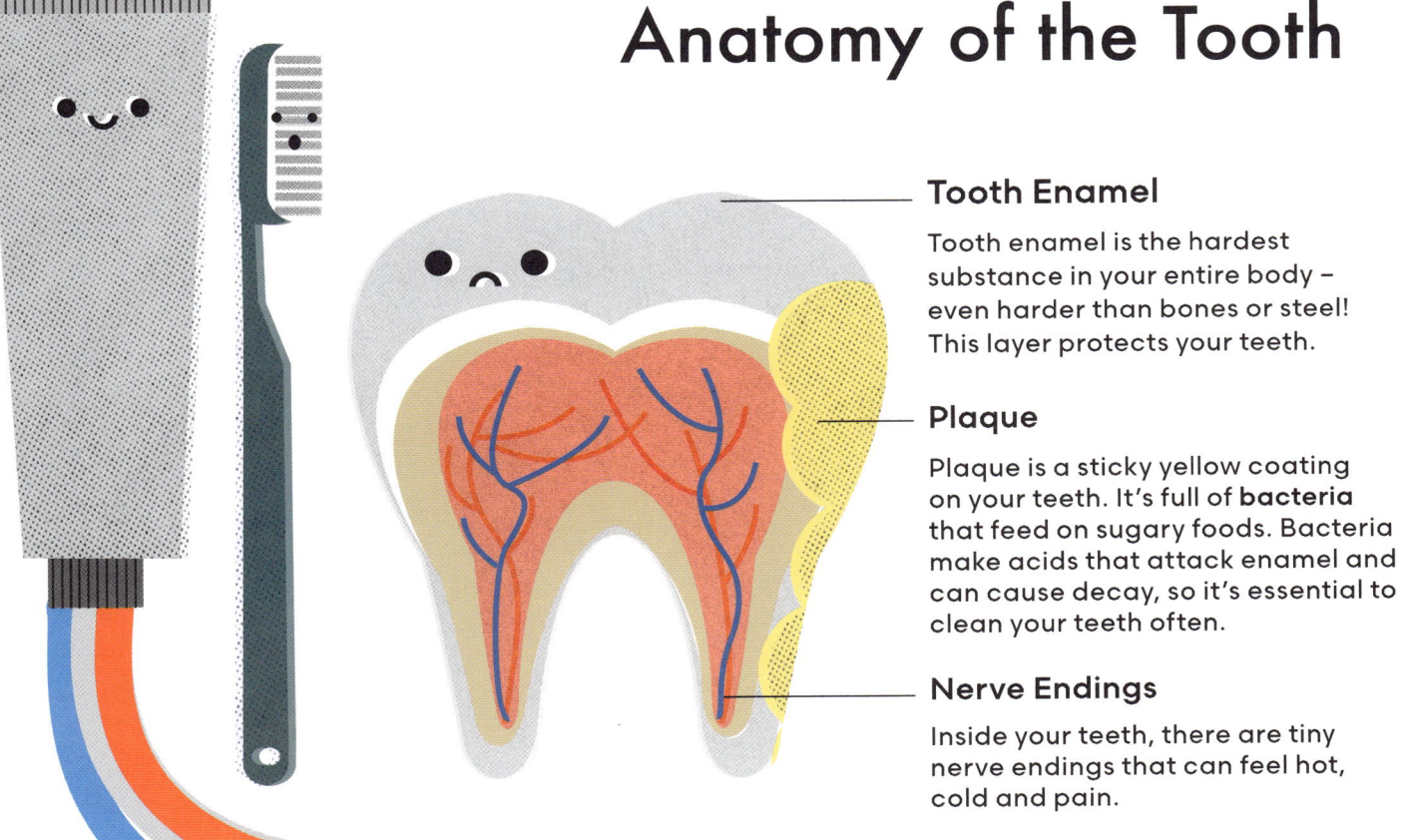

Tooth Enamel

Tooth enamel is the hardest substance in your entire body – even harder than bones or steel! This layer protects your teeth.

Plaque

Plaque is a sticky yellow coating on your teeth. It's full of **bacteria** that feed on sugary foods. Bacteria make acids that attack enamel and can cause decay, so it's essential to clean your teeth often.

Nerve Endings

Inside your teeth, there are tiny nerve endings that can feel hot, cold and pain.

Tongue

The tongue is a fascinating part of the body. It helps us eat, speak and breathe every day. The tongue also tastes food, moves it around the mouth and helps us swallow. It's very sensitive to touch and is one of the strongest muscles in the body.

The tongue lets us taste and feel things in our mouth. We can sense five basic tastes: sweet, salty, bitter, sour and umami. It also feels hot or cold **sensations**. Taste helps your brain decide what you're eating and if you like it or not!

Bitter

Bitterness is a sharp and often unpleasant taste. You can find it in foods like broccoli and olives, or in drinks like coffee.

Umami

Umami is a savoury taste that makes food taste rich. It's found in foods like mushrooms and cheese. The word 'umami' comes from Japanese and means 'tasty' or 'delicious'.

Salty

Salty tastes are often savoury. You can find this taste in foods like bacon and crisps.

Sour

Sour tastes, like lemons and pickles, are tangy and can make your mouth pucker up. Some people love the sharp flavour of sour foods.

Sweet

Sweetness is a taste that comes from sugary foods like ice cream, cakes and chocolate.

lingual tonsils

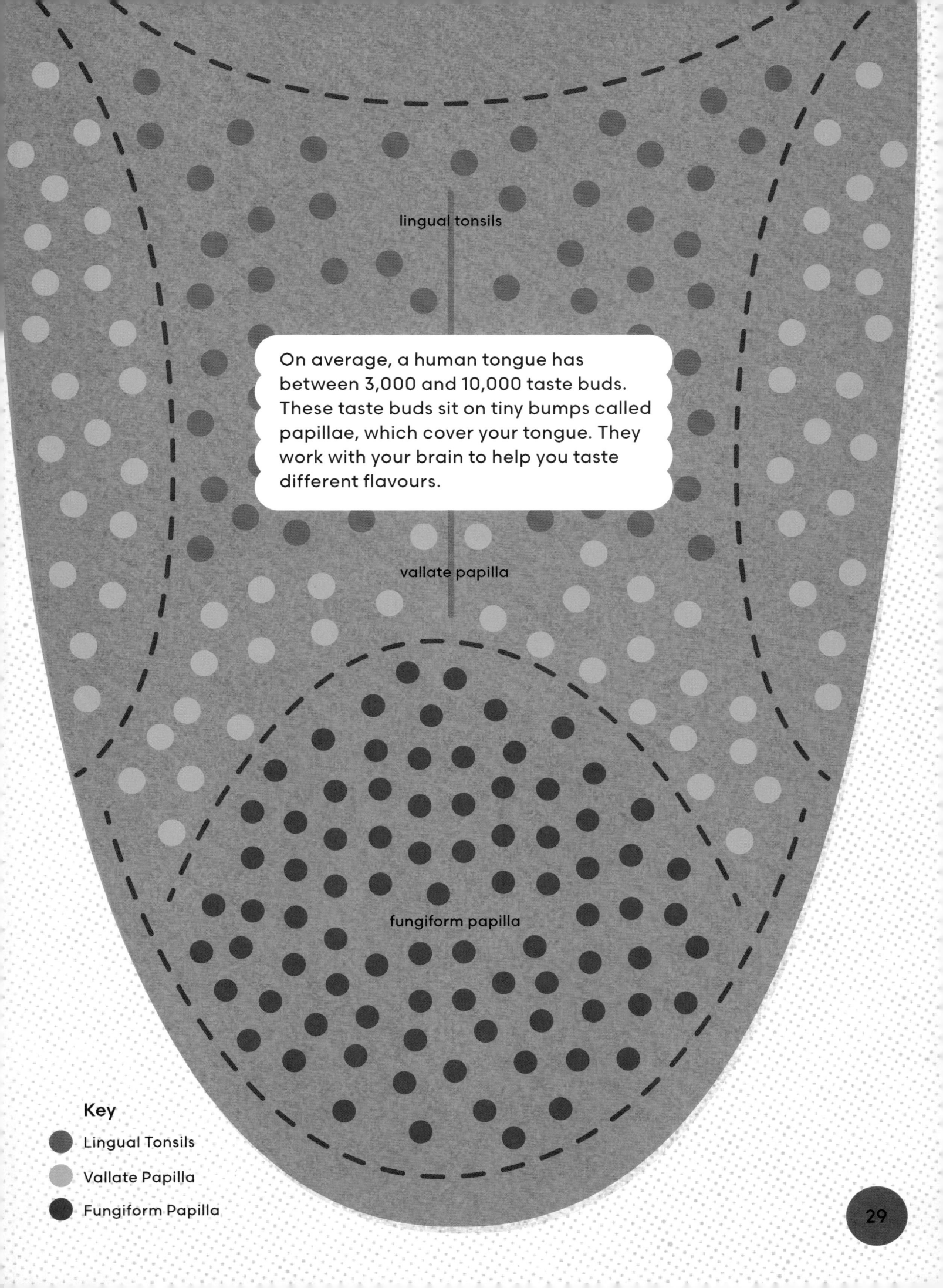

On average, a human tongue has between 3,000 and 10,000 taste buds. These taste buds sit on tiny bumps called papillae, which cover your tongue. They work with your brain to help you taste different flavours.

vallate papilla

fungiform papilla

Key
- Lingual Tonsils
- Vallate Papilla
- Fungiform Papilla

The heart beats about 60 to 80 times per minute, or 15,000 times a day. With each heart beat, the heart sends blood throughout our bodies, carrying oxygen to every cell.

Heart

Your heart is a hard-working muscle that pumps blood and oxygen around your body. It also sends waste to your lungs to be removed. Without the heart, we wouldn't live! The heart has four chambers with valves that help direct the flow of blood and each one has a special purpose.

Laughing is good for your heart! It reduces stress and gives a boost to your immune system.

Your heart is about the same size as your fist — no matter how old you are!

The heart is one of the strongest muscles in the body. Regular exercise is key to keeping your heart healthy.

30

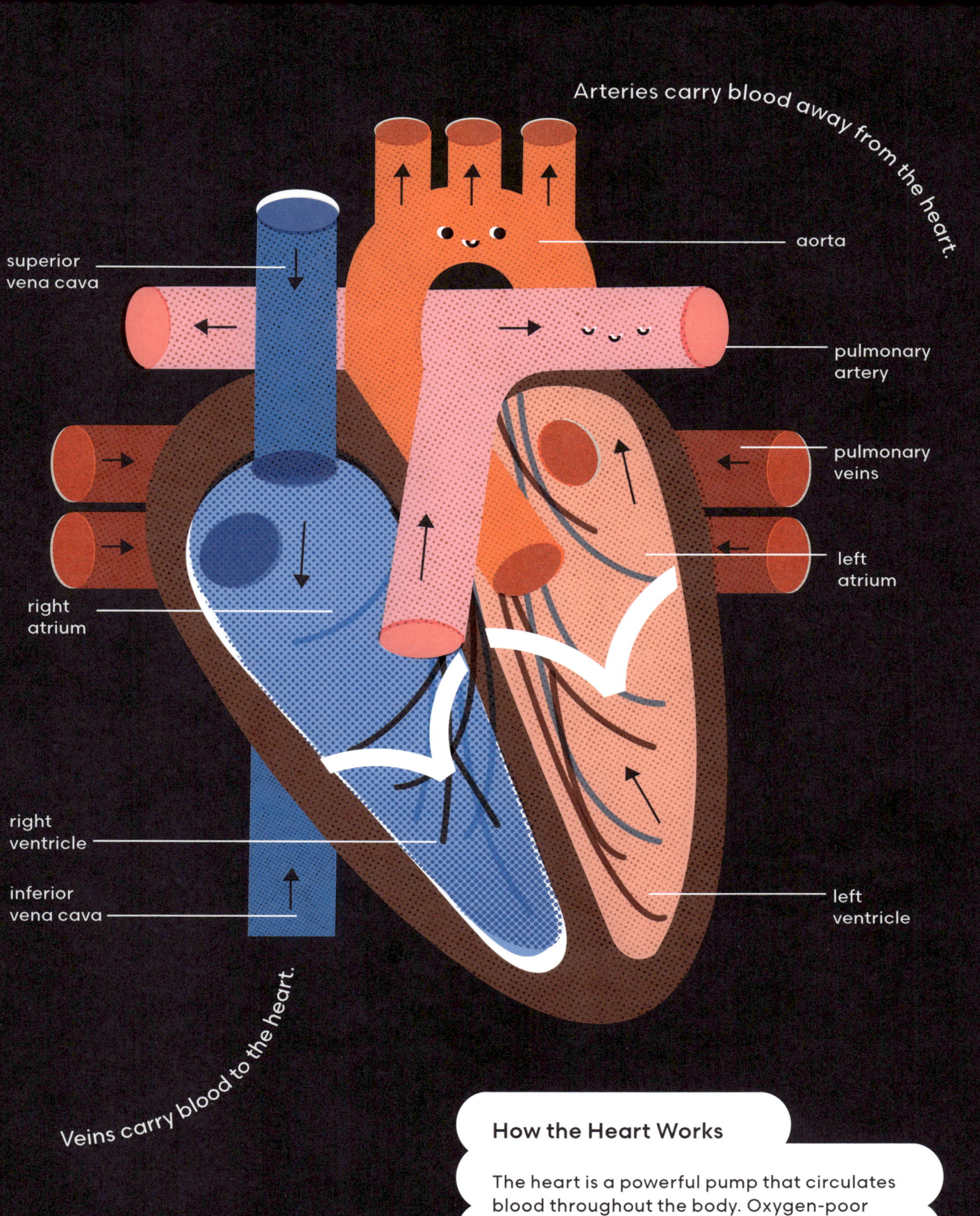

Anatomy of the Heart

- superior vena cava
- right atrium
- right ventricle
- inferior vena cava
- aorta
- pulmonary artery
- pulmonary veins
- left atrium
- left ventricle

Arteries carry blood away from the heart.

Veins carry blood to the heart.

How the Heart Works

The heart is a powerful pump that circulates blood throughout the body. Oxygen-poor blood enters the right atrium of the heart from a vein and moves into the right ventricle, which pumps it to the lungs through an artery to collect oxygen. The oxygen-rich blood then returns to the left atrium through a vein, flows into the left ventricle and finally is pumped out through an artery to supply the body.

Lungs

Lungs are organs in your chest that help you to breathe. When you breathe in, your lungs bring oxygen into your body. This oxygen moves from your lungs into your blood. When you breathe out, your lungs get rid of carbon dioxide, which is a waste gas.

The Breathing Muscle
When you breathe in, your lungs fill with air and inflate, just like a balloon. When you breathe out, your lungs get smaller and deflate as the air is released. The diaphragm, a muscle under your lungs, helps with this by moving up and down to push air in and out of your lungs.

Each day we take in around 20,000 breaths — about 7.5 million breaths each year!

When you exercise, you can breathe up to 60 times a minute to get more oxygen.

Your left lung is smaller than your right lung, to make room for your heart.

Key
1. Trachea
2. Diaphragm
3. Bronchi
4. Bronchioles
5. Alveoli
6. Lungs

How Your Lungs Work

Your lungs are like sponges that help you breathe – they are soft and full of tiny holes.

When you breathe in, your diaphragm contracts and air travels down your trachea, which then splits into two bronchi, one for each lung. These bronchi branch into smaller and smaller tubes called bronchioles, leading to tiny air sacs called alveoli. The alveoli collect oxygen your body needs and send it into your blood. Your diaphragm helps pull air in and push it out. When you breathe out, your lungs remove carbon dioxide, a waste gas your body doesn't need.

If you spread out all the tiny alveoli in your lungs, they would cover a tennis court!

Hands

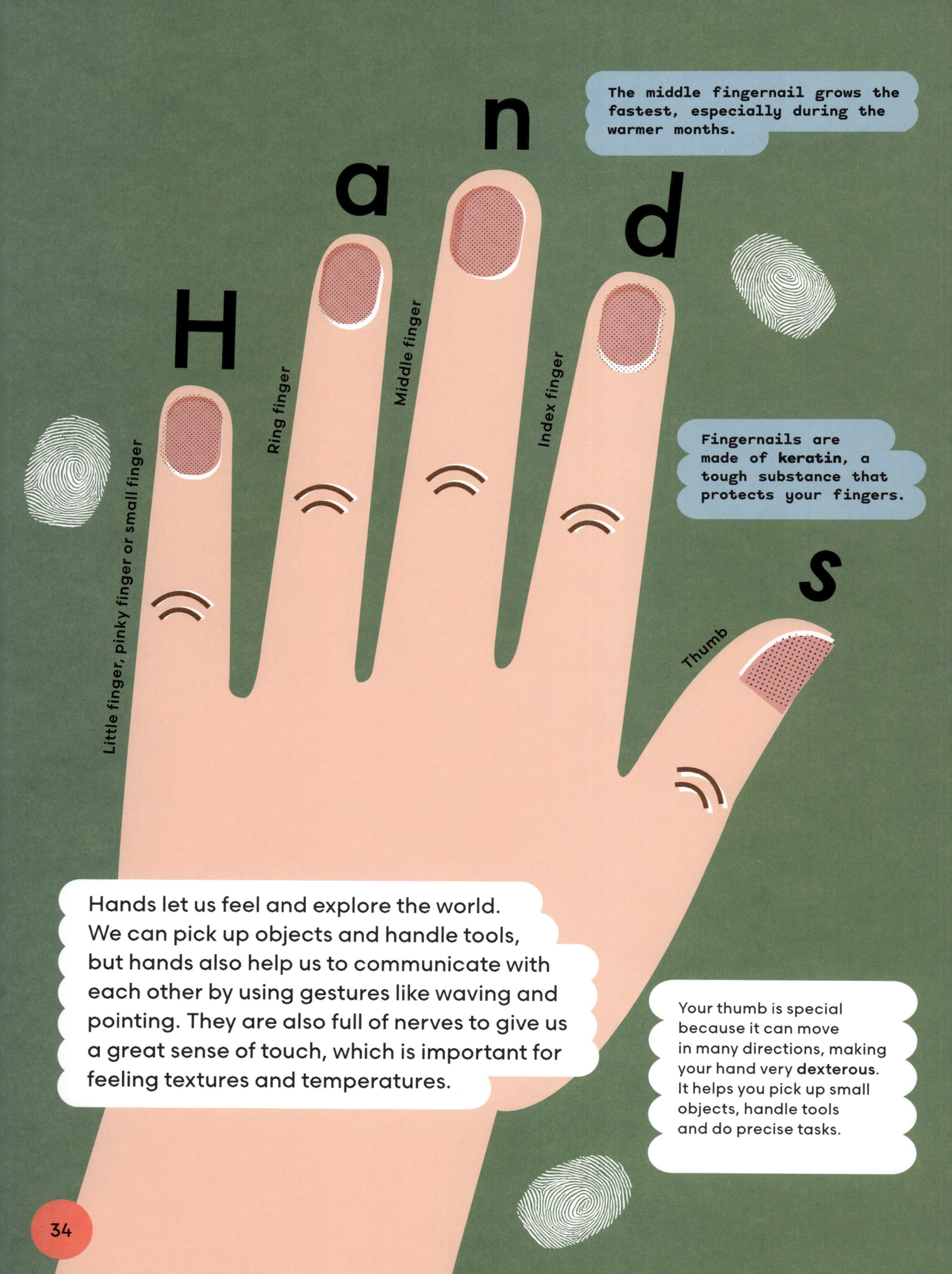

The middle fingernail grows the fastest, especially during the warmer months.

Fingernails are made of keratin, a tough substance that protects your fingers.

Little finger, pinky finger or small finger

Ring finger

Middle finger

Index finger

Thumb

Hands let us feel and explore the world. We can pick up objects and handle tools, but hands also help us to communicate with each other by using gestures like waving and pointing. They are also full of nerves to give us a great sense of touch, which is important for feeling textures and temperatures.

Your thumb is special because it can move in many directions, making your hand very **dexterous**. It helps you pick up small objects, handle tools and do precise tasks.

Handy Bones

Incredibly, just one hand contains 27 little bones. These bones give you greater flexibility and strength, helping you to do all kinds of things easily like writing, catching a ball or even tying your shoelaces!

Your fingerprints are unique to you! No one else in the world has the same fingerprints as you. They help you grip things better and feel textures more accurately.

Skin

Your skin is the largest organ of your body, covering you from head to toe! It protects you from germs, keeps your body at the right temperature and helps you feel sensations like heat, cold and pain. Your skin is always renewing itself, shedding 30,000 dead cells every minute!

Melanin

Melanin is a substance that gives colour to your hair, eyes and skin. The more melanin you produce, the darker your eyes, hair and skin will be.

Freckles

Freckles are small brown spots that appear on your skin, often when you're in the sun. They happen because your body makes extra melanin. However, freckles are not a sign of sun damage.

Thick or Thin?

Skin is its thickest on your feet (1.4mm). This thick skin helps cushion your feet when you walk, run or play. It is thinnest on your eyelids (0.5mm).

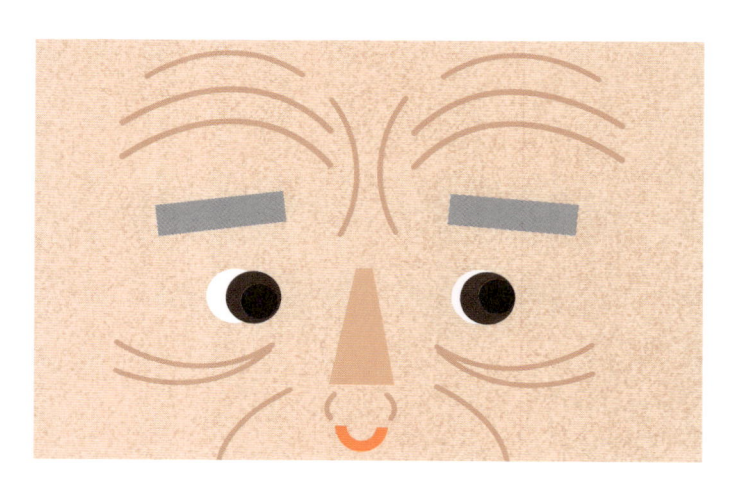

Wrinkles

Wrinkles are a natural part of getting older. They are lines and creases that mostly show on skin that is exposed to the sun such as on the face and neck. Using sun cream can help to keep wrinkles away.

Layers of Skin

Your skin has three layers that protect you, keep you warm and help you to feel things. Beneath the surface, there are hair follicles to grow hair, oil glands to keep your skin smooth, sweat glands to cool you down, **nerves** to let you feel and blood vessels to bring **nutrients**.

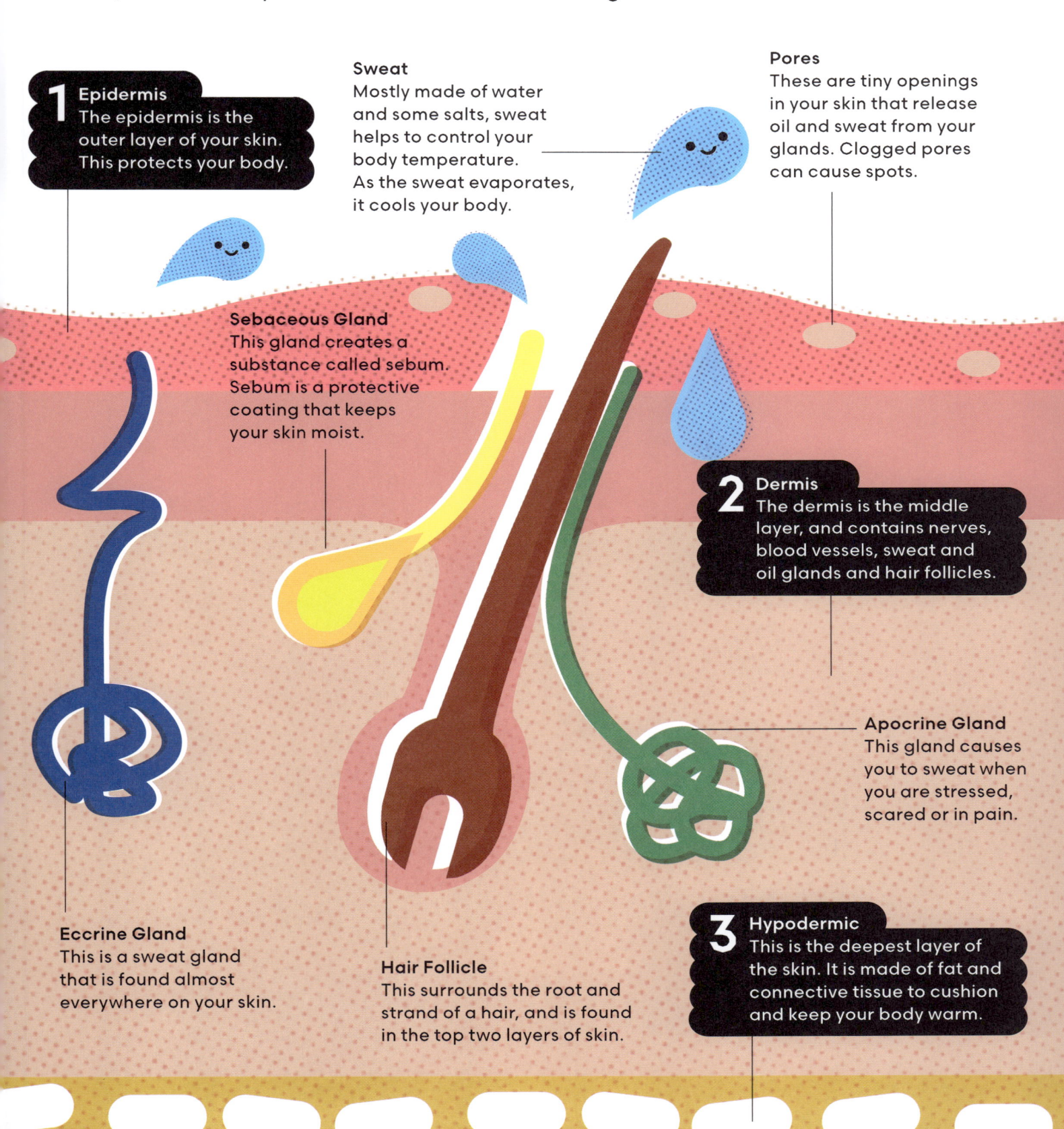

1 Epidermis
The epidermis is the outer layer of your skin. This protects your body.

Sweat
Mostly made of water and some salts, sweat helps to control your body temperature. As the sweat evaporates, it cools your body.

Pores
These are tiny openings in your skin that release oil and sweat from your glands. Clogged pores can cause spots.

Sebaceous Gland
This gland creates a substance called sebum. Sebum is a protective coating that keeps your skin moist.

2 Dermis
The dermis is the middle layer, and contains nerves, blood vessels, sweat and oil glands and hair follicles.

Apocrine Gland
This gland causes you to sweat when you are stressed, scared or in pain.

Eccrine Gland
This is a sweat gland that is found almost everywhere on your skin.

Hair Follicle
This surrounds the root and strand of a hair, and is found in the top two layers of skin.

3 Hypodermic
This is the deepest layer of the skin. It is made of fat and connective tissue to cushion and keep your body warm.

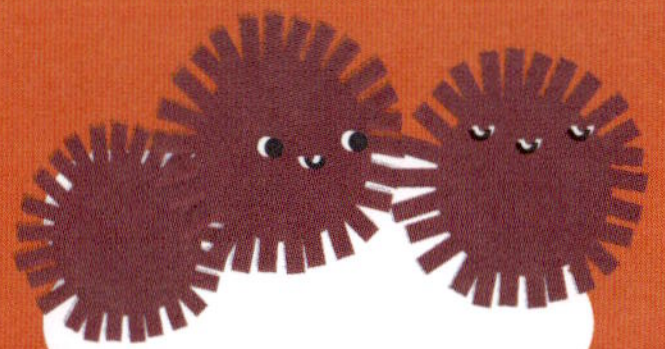

Platelets
Platelets are small cells that help to form clots to stop bleeding.

Plasma
Plasma is the liquid part of the blood in which the red and white blood cells and platelets float. It is packed with nutrients, proteins, hormones and waste products.

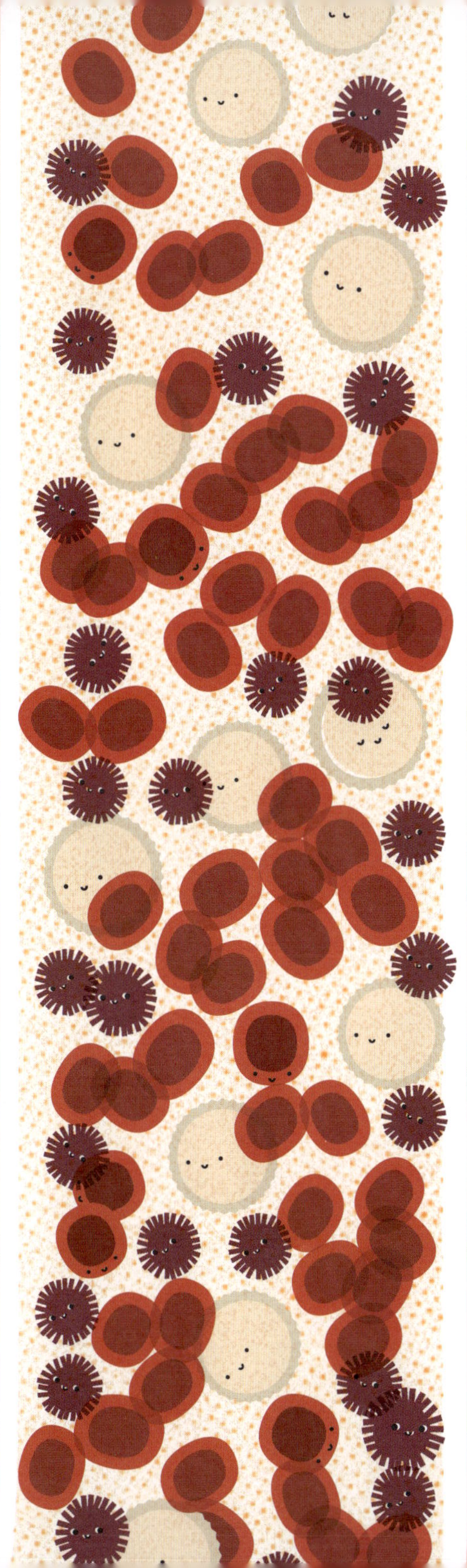

White Blood Cells
These are the biggest type of blood cell and help to protect your body from germs and fight infections.

Blood

Blood brings oxygen and nutrients to all parts of your body, fights infections with cells and antibodies, carries hormones and helps remove waste to keep your body clean.

There are three different types of blood cells (red, white and platelets). Each one has an important function. They regenerate on a regular basis to keep our bodies healthy and make sure everything is working as it should be.

On average, an adult has around five litres of blood in their body. A newborn baby only has around a quarter of a litre.

Blood comes in different shades of red. Bright red blood is full of oxygen, while dark red blood has less oxygen (usually found in the veins). There are four main blood types: A, B, AB and O. Each type can be positive (+) or negative (-), which refers to a special type of protein found on the surface of red blood cells. AB- is the rarest type of the main groups.

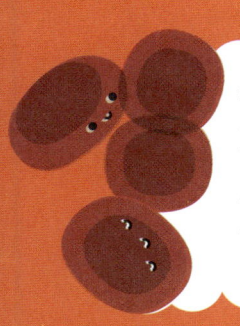

Red Blood Cells
These cells carry oxygen from the lungs to the rest of the body.

39

Kidneys and Bladder

Kidneys are bean-shaped organs, each about the size of a fist. They are amazing filters that remove waste and extra liquid from your blood, keeping your body clean and healthy. Located just below your ribcage with one on each side of your **spine**, these important organs work hard to keep you feeling good.

Urine Colour Chart

Your kidneys can change the colour of your urine based on how much water you drink. When you drink plenty of water, your urine is pale yellow or clear, showing you're hydrated. If you don't drink enough, it becomes darker yellow because your body is saving water. Staying hydrated helps your kidneys flush out waste and keeps your body healthy!

1. Over hydrated, hold off for a little while.
2. Hydrated, keep going!
3. You're still well hydrated!
4. Mildly dehydrated, drink more water.
5. Drink more water, you're dehydrated!

Bladder

The bladder holds pee. As it fills up, it expands like a balloon. When the bladder fills with about 270ml of pee (which is about as much as a 7-year-old can hold), nerves in your bladder signal to your brain that it's time to go to the toilet. Your bladder grows as your body grows.

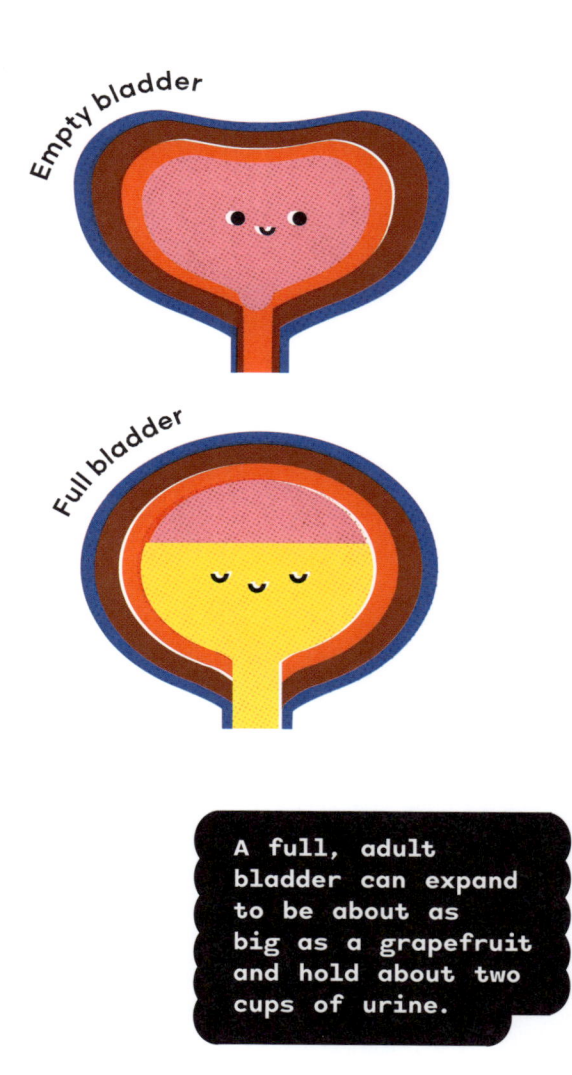

Empty bladder

Full bladder

Did you know? Your kidneys also help to control your blood pressure because they need just the right pressure to work properly.

A full, adult bladder can expand to be about as big as a grapefruit and hold about two cups of urine.

Urinary System

How the Urinary System Works

The kidneys remove salt, **toxins**, waste and extra water from your blood to make pee (urine). The urine then travels from your kidneys to your bladder through thin tubes called ureters. Once the urine reaches your bladder, it is stored there until you are ready to pee! A muscle called a sphincter holds the urine in until it's time to go. When you're ready, the sphincter relaxes, and the urine leaves your body through a tube called the urethra.

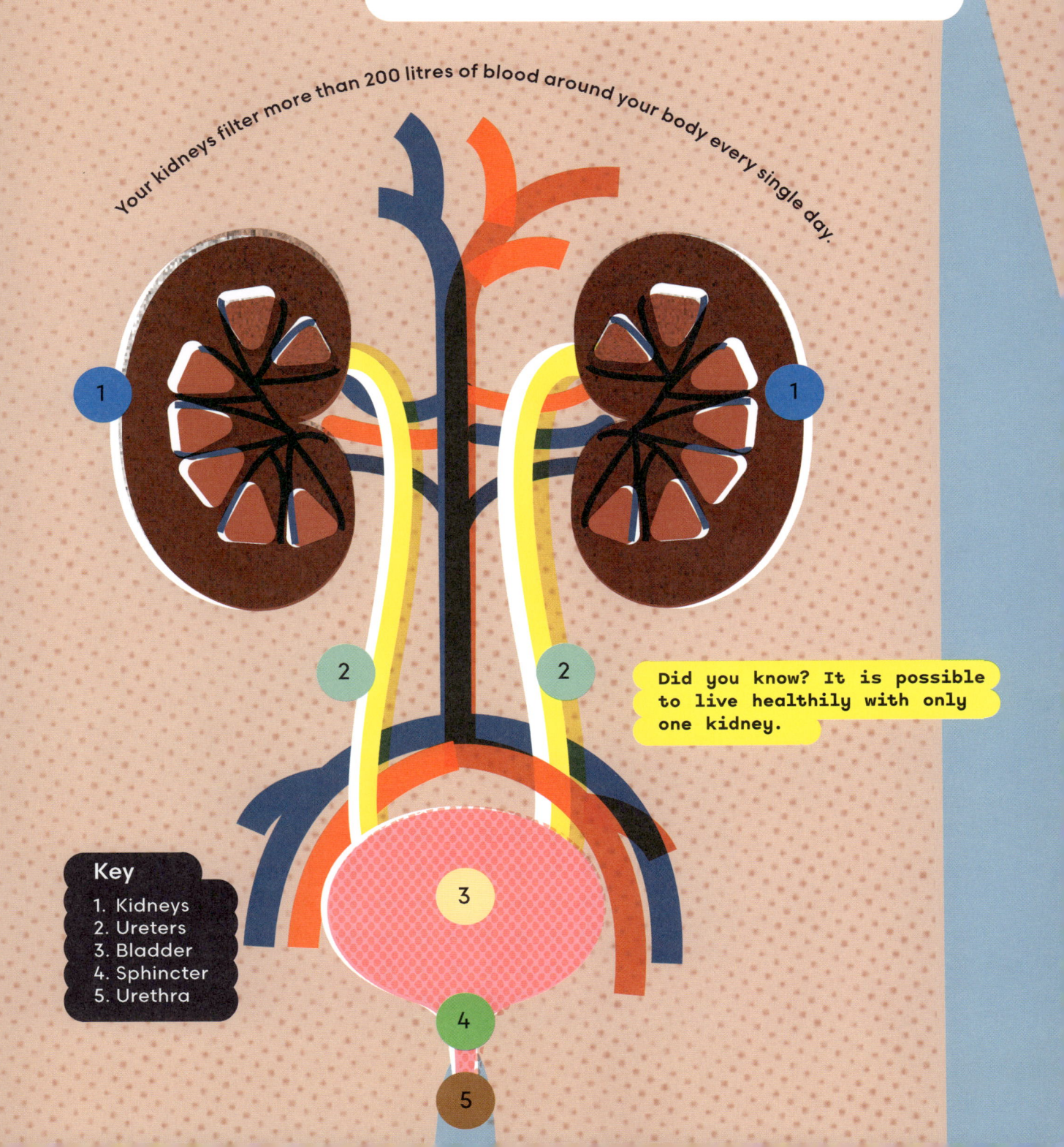

Your kidneys filter more than 200 litres of blood around your body every single day.

Did you know? It is possible to live healthily with only one kidney.

Key
1. Kidneys
2. Ureters
3. Bladder
4. Sphincter
5. Urethra

Your stomach muscles mix and churn the food to help break it down, while the stomach lining protects it

Key
1. Food pipe
2. Stomach lining
3. Muscle in stomach wall
4. Stomach
5. Food
6. Duodenum

Stomach

The stomach is a very important organ in your tummy. It is part of the digestive system and helps to break down the food you eat. When food reaches your stomach, it contracts and produces acids and enzymes that break down food. Your stomach also stores food for a while before passing it into the intestine for further digestion.

Digestive System

The digestive system consists of the parts of the body that work together to turn food and liquids into the building blocks and fuel that the body needs. The organs that take in food and liquids break them down into substances that the body can use for energy, growth and tissue repair. Waste leaves the body through bowel movements.

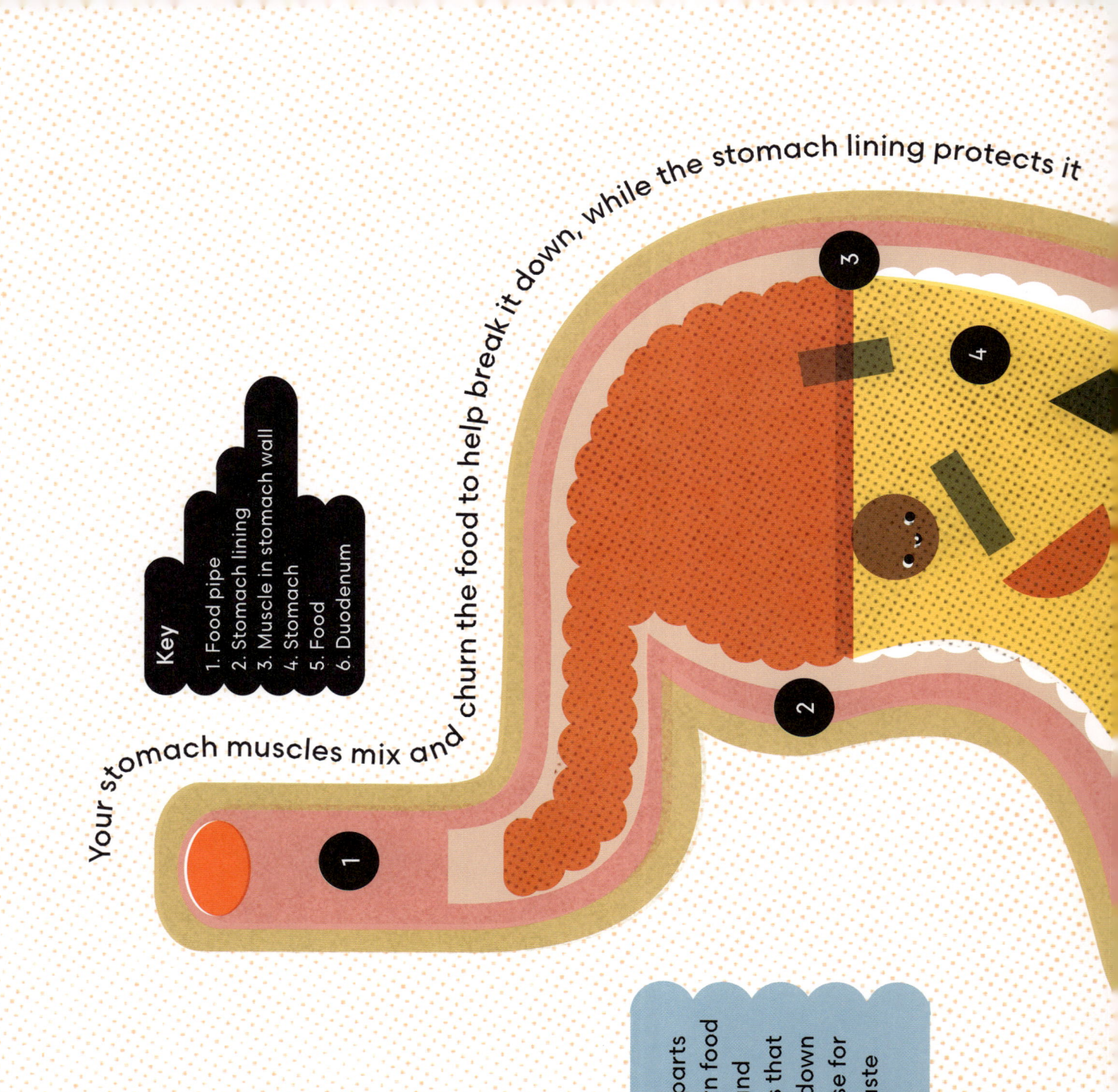

from the strong acids used for digestion.

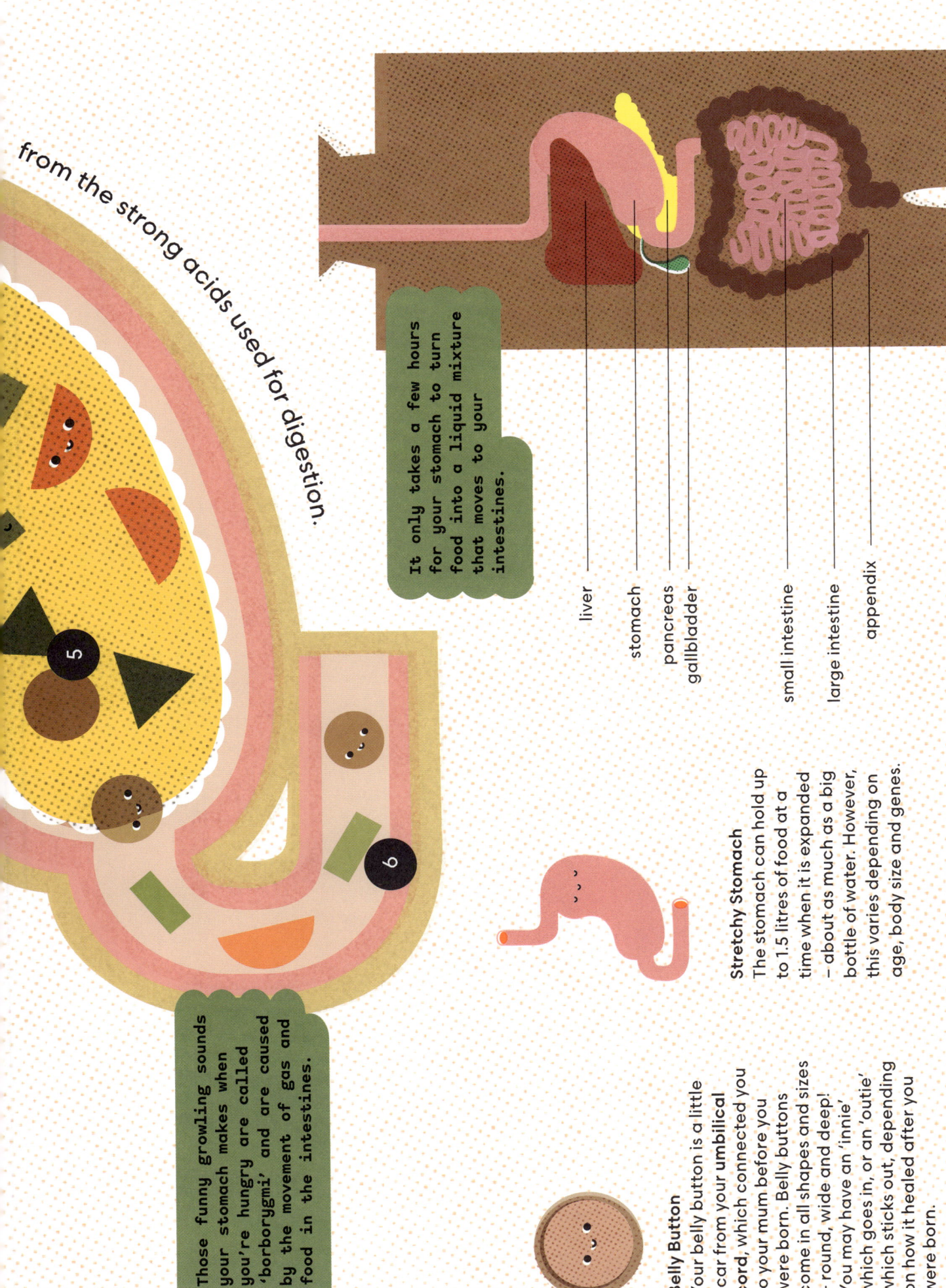

It only takes a few hours for your stomach to turn food into a liquid mixture that moves to your intestines.

liver
stomach
pancreas
gallbladder
small intestine
large intestine
appendix

Those funny growling sounds your stomach makes when you're hungry are called 'borborygmi' and are caused by the movement of gas and food in the intestines.

Stretchy Stomach
The stomach can hold up to 1.5 litres of food at a time when it is expanded – about as much as a big bottle of water. However, this varies depending on age, body size and genes.

Belly Button
Your belly button is a little scar from your umbilical cord, which connected you to your mum before you were born. Belly buttons come in all shapes and sizes – round, wide and deep! You may have an 'innie' which goes in, or an 'outie' which sticks out, depending on how it healed after you were born.

43

Liver and Pancreas

Key
1. Liver
2. Stomach
3. Gallbladder
4. Pancreas
5. Large intestine
6. Small intestine
7. Appendix
8. Rectum

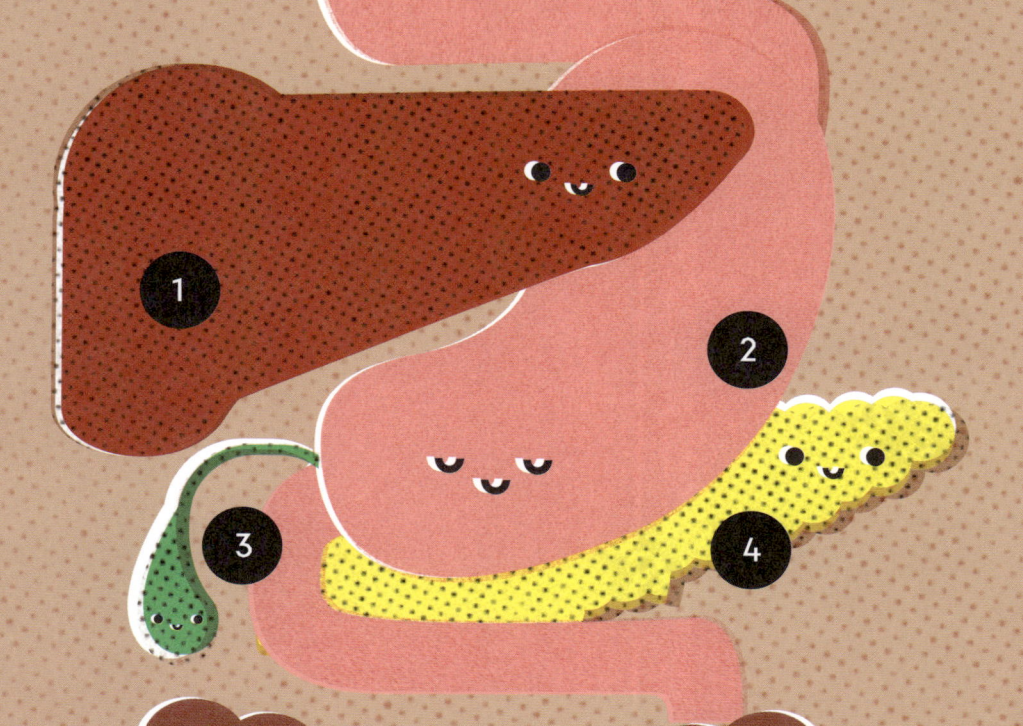

> The appendix is a tiny pouch on the large intestine. It once helped digest tough plants but became less needed. Now, it may store good bacteria and support the immune system!

The Digestive System

44

The liver and pancreas are a great team! The liver helps clean your blood by removing toxins and turning food into energy. The pancreas helps control your **blood sugar levels**, making sure they are not too high and not too low.

```
The liver is your
biggest internal organ.
In adults, it is about
the same size as an
American football!
```

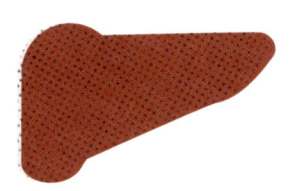

Liver

The liver has several important roles. It removes harmful substances from the blood to keep your body clean and healthy. It also produces bile, a yellow-green liquid that helps you to digest fats and absorb vitamins. The liver also saves extra sugar from food and stores it as energy. When your body needs it, the liver releases the sugar to keep you going!

Pancreas

The pancreas sits behind the stomach and makes **enzymes** that are important for digestion. It also makes hormones such as **insulin** which helps our body use sugar for energy. Without insulin, your body can't get energy from the food you eat.

If the pancreas doesn't make enough insulin or if the body can't use insulin properly, it can lead to diabetes. People with diabetes need to manage their blood sugar levels carefully.

```
The pancreas is about 15cm
long and shaped like a
flat pear.
```

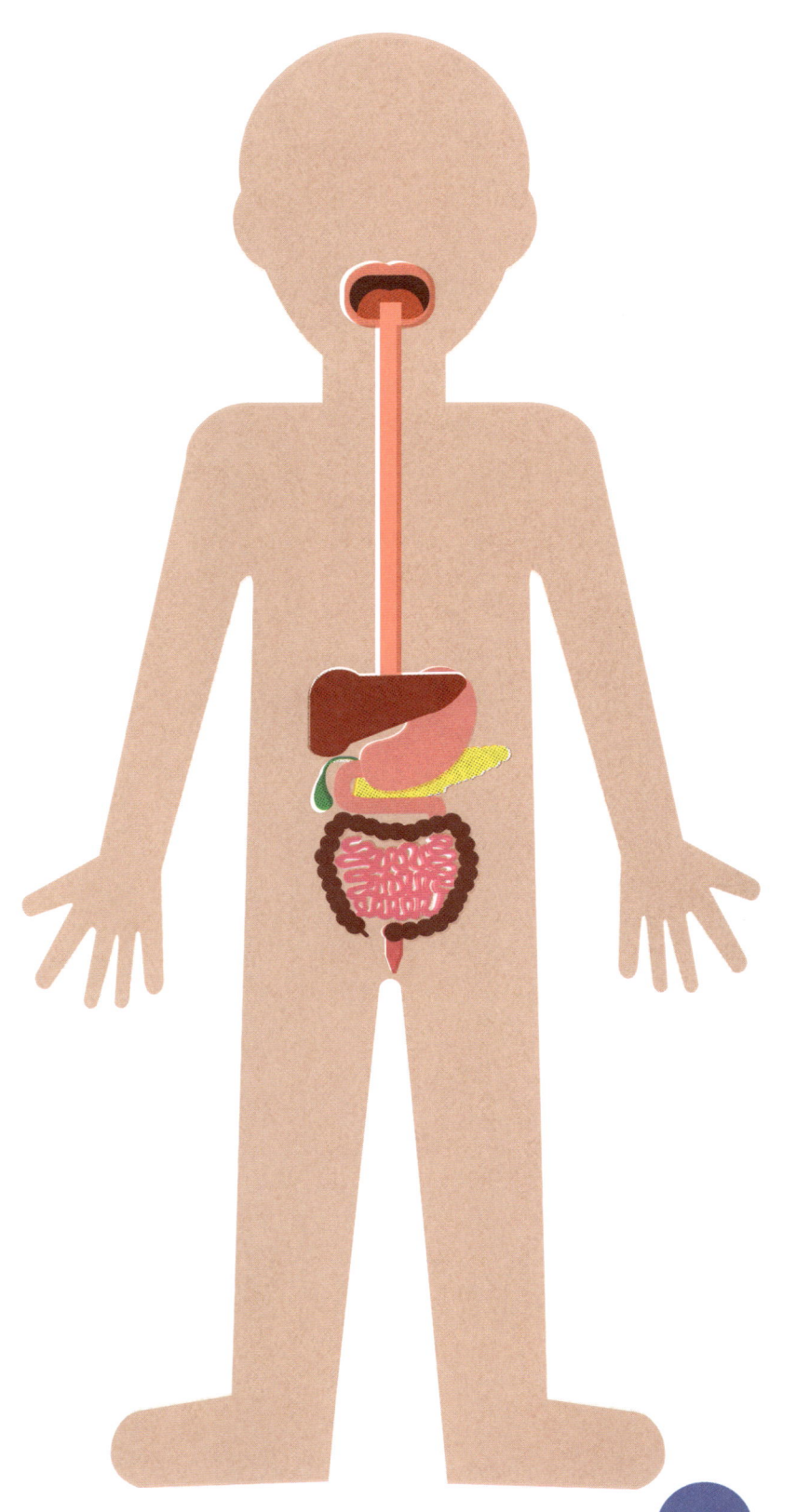

45

Intestines

The intestines are a key part of our digestive system. They help us turn the food we eat into energy and nutrients. As food travels through the intestines, it gets broken down so our bodies can use all the good stuff. Any leftover waste is then pushed out of the body.

Once you have eaten, it takes about six to eight hours for food to travel through your stomach and small intestine. Then, the food moves into your large intestine, where it is further digested. The waste is then separated to be removed as pee (urine) and poo (faeces).

Large Intestine

This tube collects waste from the food digested in the small intestine. It absorbs water and salts, turning the waste into solid poo. The large intestine also has friendly bacteria that help break down any leftover food. Muscles in its walls move in waves to push the poo towards the rectum.

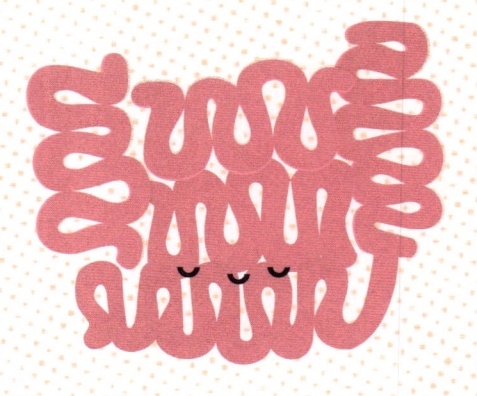

Small Intestine

The small intestine connects to the large intestine. Its wall absorbs **nutrients**, vitamins and salts from food, which then enter the bloodstream and travel to the body's organs.

`It takes about 36 hours for food to pass through the whole large intestine.`

`Despite its name, the small intestine is almost 6 metres long and very stretchy!`

The Bristol Stool Chart

Your poo can be different colours depending on what you eat. For example, eating lots of spinach can make your poo green, and blueberries can cause your poo to turn black!

Poo can come in different shapes and sizes too. The way your poo looks and smells can tell a lot about your health. Doctors use the Bristol Stool Chart to check if your poo is healthy. It categorises poo into seven different types.

1 Small Hard Lumps
This suggests constipation.

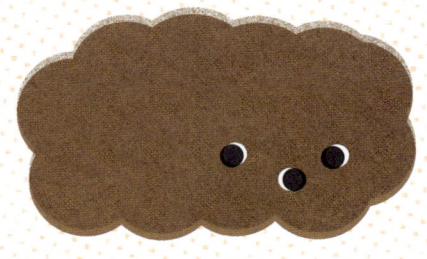

2 Lumpy
This suggests you may be slightly constipated.

3 Smooth and Soft with Cracks
This is normal and healthy.

4 Soft Sausage
This is normal and the ideal poo shape!

5 Soft Blobs
This suggests you may have mild diarrhoea or are lacking in fibre.

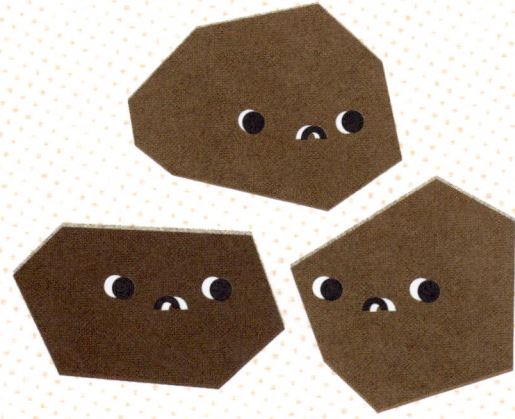

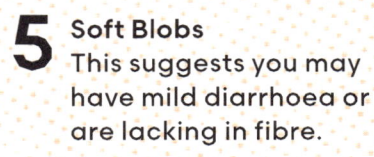

6 Mushy and Ragged
This suggests you may have mild diarrhoea.

7 Liquid
You definitely have diarrhoea!

Cells and Production

Cells are tiny building blocks that make up our body. The human body has millions of cells! They are so small you need a **microscope** to see them. They give our body its shape, take in nutrients from food, and turn those nutrients into energy so we can move and grow. Inside each cell is something special called DNA, which holds the instructions that make you unique. Cells are the beginning of life.

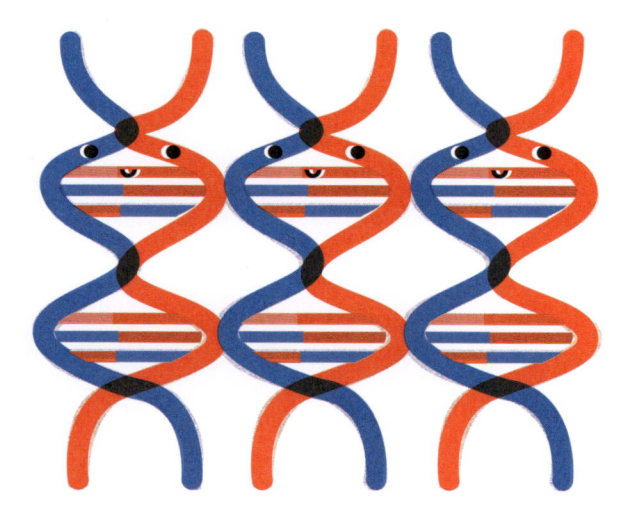

What Makes Me, Me?

DNA, or deoxyribonucleic acid, is like a special code that makes you who you are. It holds all your genetic information, which is passed on from your parents. DNA looks like a twisting ladder and contains all the blueprints for how your body works.

Reproductive Organs

Men and women have different reproductive organs. A woman's ovaries produce egg cells, and her uterus can carry a developing baby. During **puberty**, the body changes and matures so that a person can eventually have children.

Male
The male reproductive system includes the testicles (which produce sperm), penis, prostate, vas deferens and urethra.

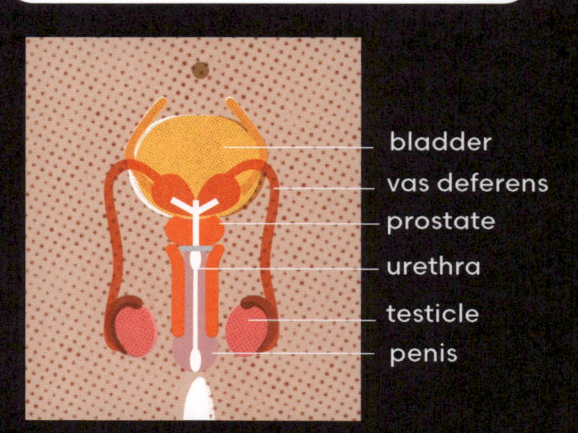

- bladder
- vas deferens
- prostate
- urethra
- testicle
- penis

Female
The female reproductive system consists of the ovaries (which produce eggs), fallopian tubes, uterus, cervix and vagina.

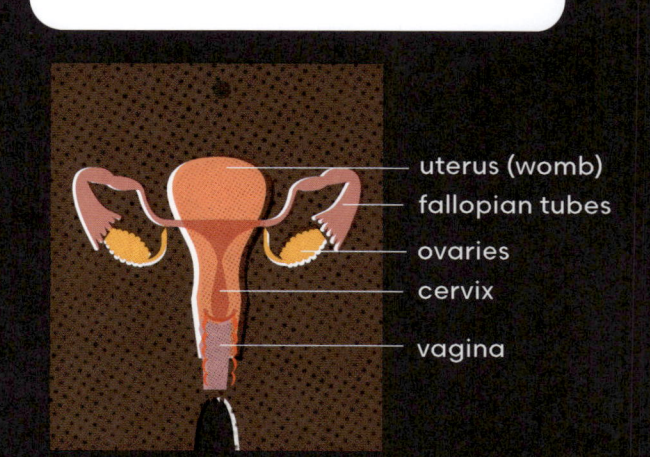

- uterus (womb)
- fallopian tubes
- ovaries
- cervix
- vagina

> You shed millions of skin cells every day, but don't worry! New skin cells are constantly being made to replace the old ones.

Egg
Jelly coat
Cytoplasm
Nucleus

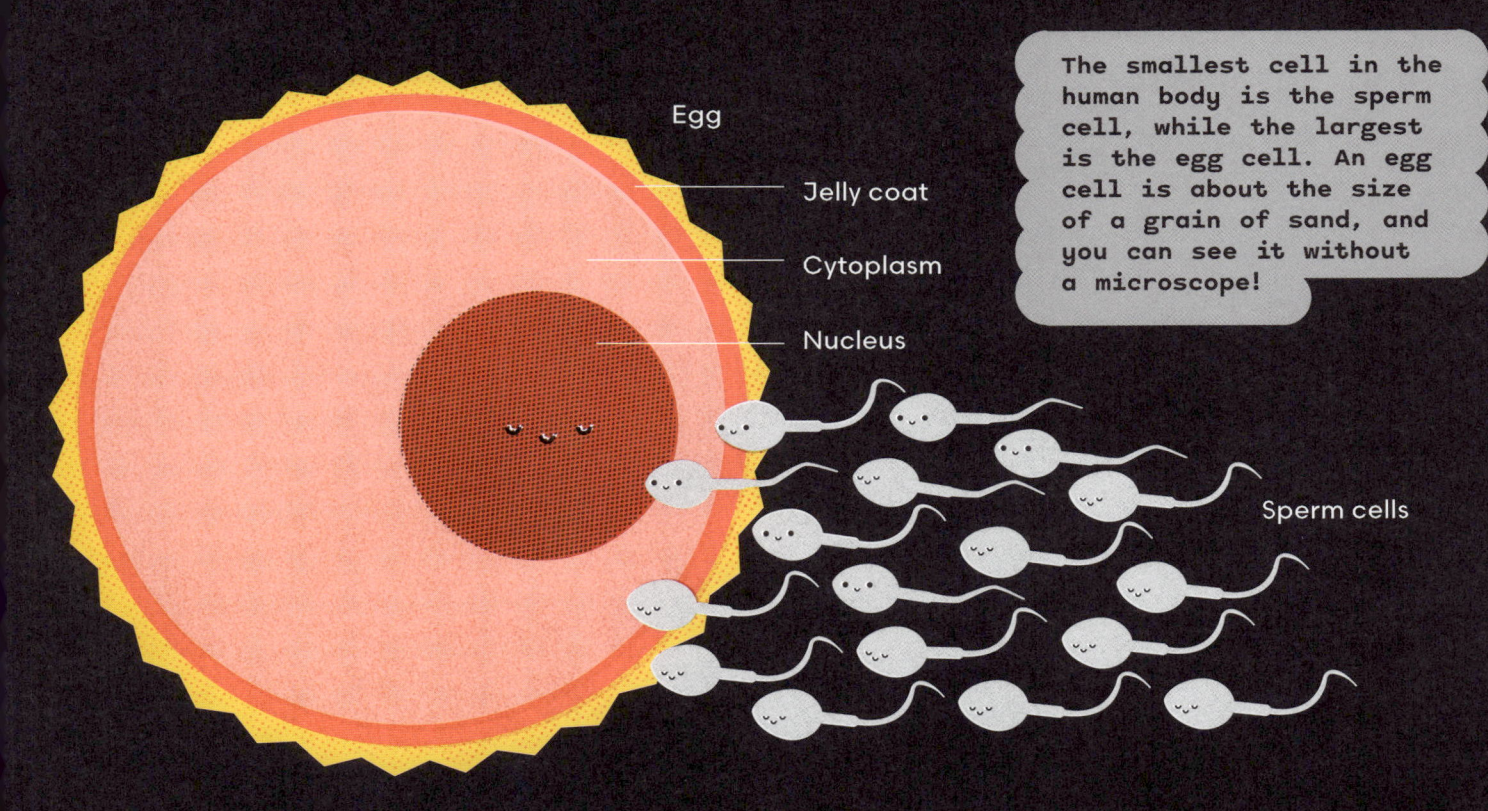

Sperm cells

The smallest cell in the human body is the sperm cell, while the largest is the egg cell. An egg cell is about the size of a grain of sand, and you can see it without a microscope!

How Was I Made?

A baby is made when a special cell from a man, called a sperm, joins with a special cell from a woman, called an egg. The sperm comes from the man's testicle and the egg comes from the woman's ovary. This joining happens inside the woman's body, in the fallopian tube which leads to the uterus. The combined cells grow and divide, forming a tiny baby. The baby gets half of its DNA from its mum and half from its dad, which is why it may look like both parents. Over about nine months, the baby grows bigger until it's ready to be born.

Key
1. Placenta
2. Umbilical cord
3. Foetus
4. Uterus
5. Cervix

Muscles and Tendons

Muscles are found all over our body and are part of the muscular system. There are over 600 muscles in your body! They help you move, pump blood and control your heartbeat, breathing and digestion. Muscles give you strength and flexibility, so you can do things like walk, run, dance and cycle. Tendons are like strong ropes that connect your muscles to your bones, helping you to move smoothly and powerfully.

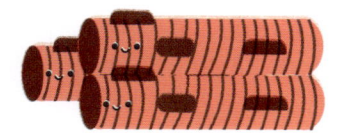

Skeletal muscles

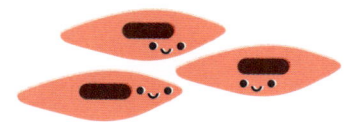

Smooth muscles

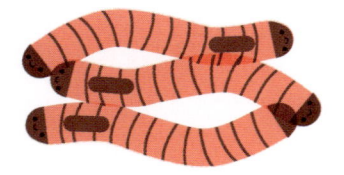

Cardiac (heart) muscles

Muscles

Muscles lie under your skin and are made up of thousands of stretchy fibres. Each of these fibres is wrapped in a thin, see-through layer called a perimysium. There are three types of muscles that help your body move and work properly.

How Do Muscles Work?

Muscles work in pairs by contracting and relaxing. When you want to move, your brain sends a message to your muscles. Some muscles contract, making them shorter and tighter, while others relax and get longer. This contracting and relaxing helps your body move, like when you lift your arm or kick a ball.

Some high protein foods can help you build muscle mass more quickly than other foods. These include eggs, meat, yoghurt, milk and beans.

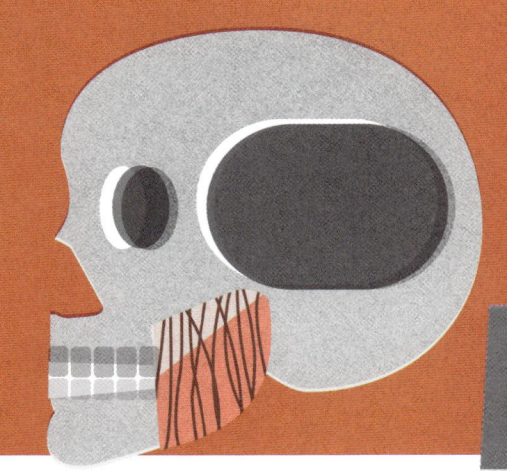

The strongest muscle in the body is the masseter. This is the chewing muscle that lifts your jaw. It can close your teeth with a force as strong as 25kg, making it powerful enough to help you bite and chew food.

Your heart is a hard-working muscle that beats thousands of times a day. It moves on its own, without us thinking about it.

Muscles
Muscles are made up of thousands of stretchy fibres.

Tendons
Tendons are soft tissues that connect muscle to bone. They absorb some of the impact from your muscles when you do things like running or jumping.

Cartilage
Cartilage is a tough, flexible tissue found in many parts of your body like the nose, ears and between your bones. It cushions joints, helps them move smoothly and protects bones from rubbing against each other.

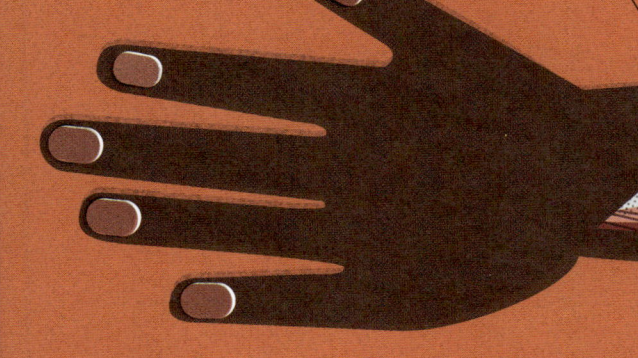

Bones and Joints

Your body has a skeleton made up of 206 bones. This skeleton not only gives your body its shape, but also protects your organs and helps you move. Bones grow a lot when you're a child and a teenager, but they keep changing and repairing themselves all the time. Inside your bones is something called **bone marrow**, which makes new blood cells to keep you healthy.

What Are Bones Made Of?

Bones are made of protein, **collagen**, and minerals, especially calcium. The calcium makes bones hard and strong, while the collagen makes them flexible, so they don't break easily. This mix helps your bones stay tough but also a little bendy, so they can handle lots of movement and pressure.

Joints

Joints are places where two bones meet. There are six types of freely movable **synovial** joints.

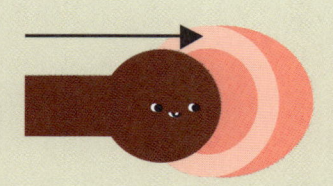

1. **Ball and Socket**
   This joint allows movement in all directions, like in your shoulder and hip.

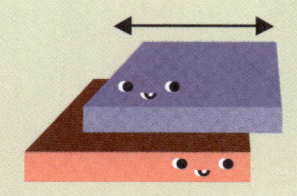

2. **Gliding**
   These joints are in your wrists and ankles, letting bones slide over each other.

3. **Hinge**
   Found in your elbows and knees, these joints move like a door opening and closing.

4. **Condyloid**
   These joints are found in your fingers, allowing them to bend but not twist.

5. **Pivot**
   Found in your neck, the pivot joint allows you to turn your head from side to side.

6. **Saddle**
   Found in your thumb, this joint allows back-and-forth and side-to-side movement.

52

The Skeleton

1. Skull
2. **Ossicles** (ear bones)
3. **Clavicle** (collarbone)
4. **Scapula** (shoulder blade)
5. **Ribcage**
6. **Humerus**
7. **Radius**
8. **Ulna**
9. **Spine** (vertebrae)
10. **Pelvis**
11. **Phalanges** (in hands and feet)
12. Femur
13. **Patella** (kneecap)
14. **Fibula**
15. **Tibia**
16. **Tarsals**
17. **Metatarsals**
18. **Carpals** (wrist bones)
19. **Metacarpals**
20. **Sternum** (breastbone)

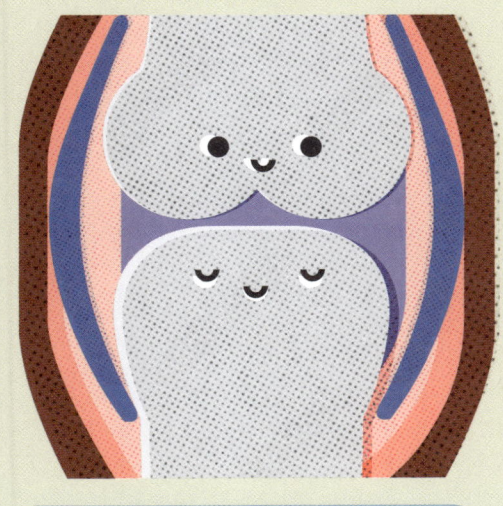

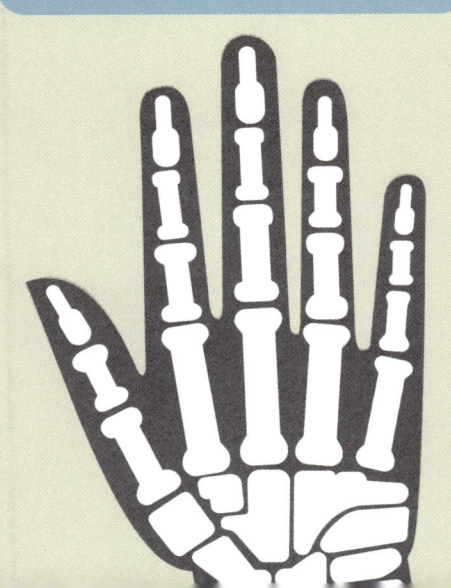

Your smallest bone is in your ear! The stapes (or stirrup bone) in your ear is the tiniest bone in your body — it's smaller than a grain of rice!

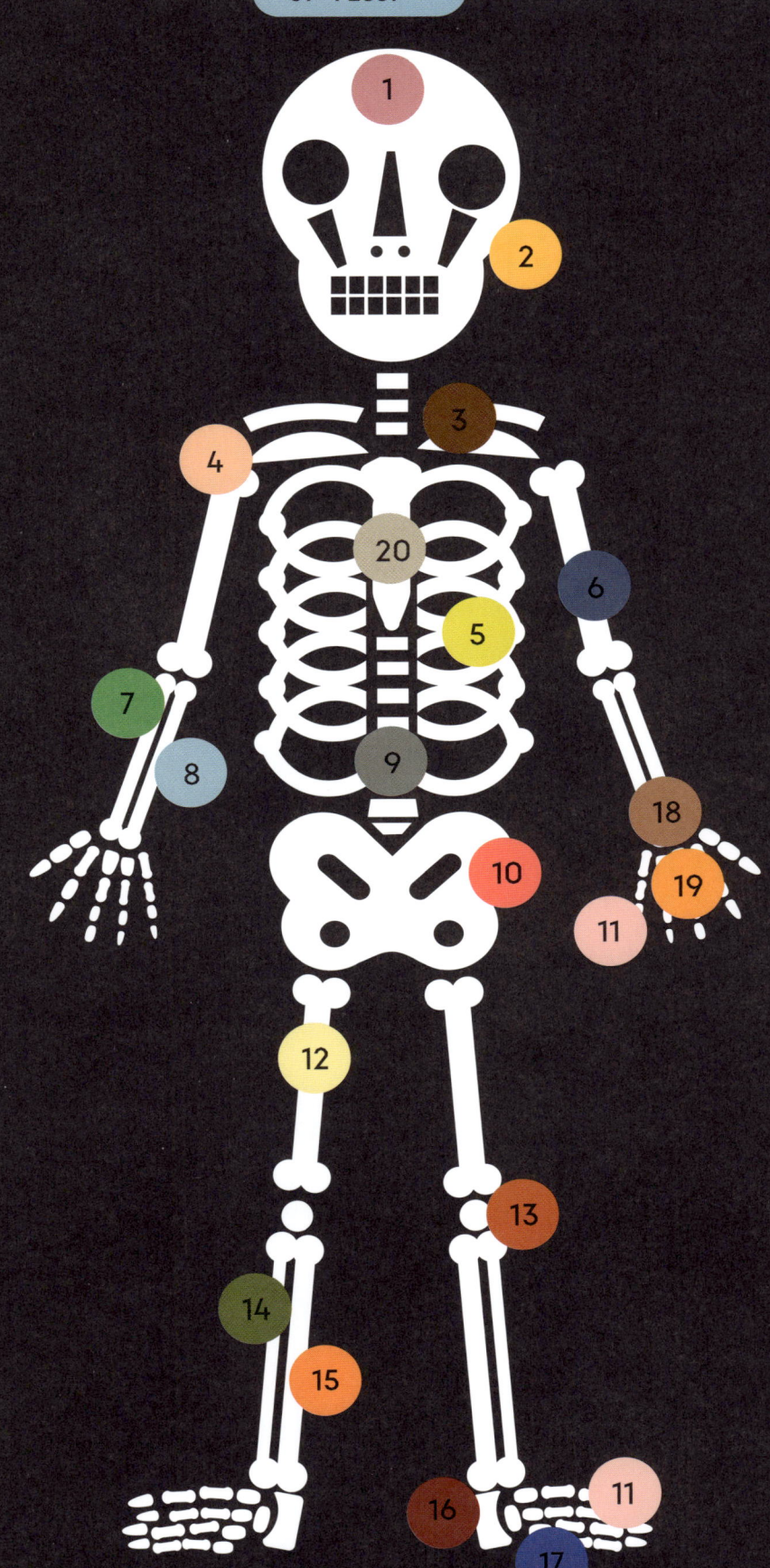

Your bones are alive! Bones may feel hard, but they are living tissue that grows, repairs and produces blood cells.

Feet

We're now at the bottom of the body! The feet are the foundation of your entire body, making them super important as they support your whole body weight. They help with balance, posture, mobility and your overall well-being.

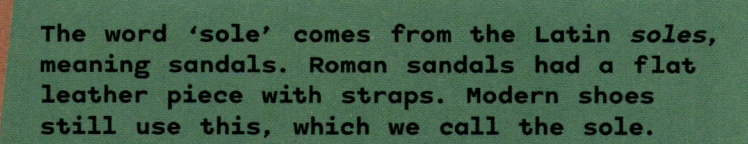

The word 'sole' comes from the Latin *soles*, meaning sandals. Roman sandals had a flat leather piece with straps. Modern shoes still use this, which we call the sole.

Ticklish Toes

There are thousands of nerve endings in your feet, making them very sensitive! This sensitivity helps you feel the ground and keep your balance. Because your feet are so sensitive, they can be very ticklish too!

54

Each foot has 26 bones, 33 joints and over 100 ligaments, muscles and tendons!

Funky Feet

The feet sweat more than other parts of the body. They each have around 250,000 sweat glands! This helps keep them cool, especially since they are often enclosed in socks and shoes. Feet can sometimes smell cheesy because sweat creates a moist environment where bacteria love to grow. These bacteria produce a strong smell, so wash your feet often, especially between the toes!

Mighty Big Toe

The big toe is bigger than the other toes and has more muscles attached because it bears more weight. Unlike the other toes, it has only two joints instead of three, giving it extra stability.

Head to Toe

We've now explored all the parts of our body, from head to toe! The human body is truly amazing. Each part, from organs to systems, is carefully organised to work together, allowing us to move, think, breathe and grow. No part can work alone – they all depend on each other.

What's your favourite thing you've learned about your body?

Systems

There are 10 major body systems that include the skeletal, muscular, respiratory, digestive, nervous, circulatory, endocrine, lymphatic, urinary and reproductive system. Below are six of them.

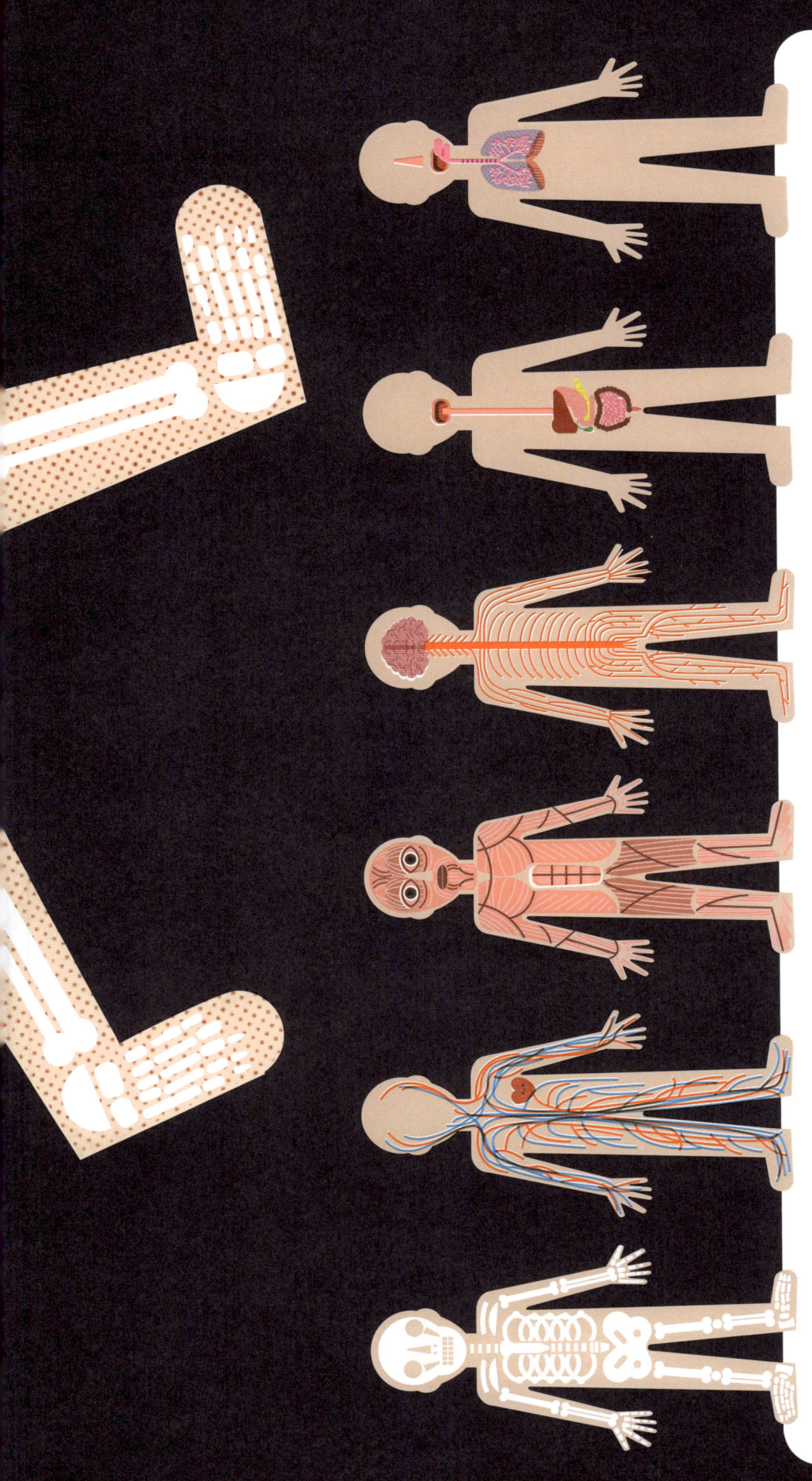

Skeletal
The skeletal system gives your body its shape, allows movement, creates blood cells and protects your organs.

Circulatory
The circulatory system delivers nutrients and oxygen to all the cells in your body. It consists of the heart and blood vessels.

Muscular
The muscular system is made of muscle fibres attached to bones or internal organs and blood vessels. It is responsible for movement.

Nervous
The nervous system includes the brain, **spinal cord** and a network of nerves. It sends messages between the brain and the body.

Digestive
The digestive system is a group of organs that work together to turn food into nutrients. It includes your gallbladder, liver, pancreas and digestive tract.

Respiratory
Your respiratory system is responsible for breathing. It is made up of your lungs, airways, diaphragm, voice box, throat, nose and mouth.

Body Facts

Here are some mind-blowing facts about how your body works!

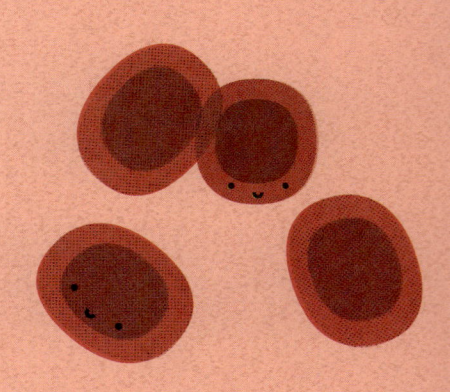

The fastest muscle in the human body is the orbicularis oculi, the muscle responsible for blinking. It can contract in as little as 10 milliseconds!

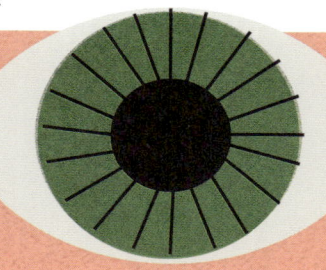

On average, men have about 5.5 litres of blood in their bodies, while women have about 4.5 litres.

The span of your arms stretched out at your sides is about equal to your height.

The large intestine is about 1.5 metres long. If you stretched out your large intestine, it would be about as long as the width of a queen-size bed.

The funny bone is a nerve that runs along the outside of your elbow. When it is banged, or rubs up against one of the bones in your upper arms, it creates a strange burning or tingling sensation which gives it its name.

The body has 2.5 million sweat pores.

Your brain doesn't feel pain!

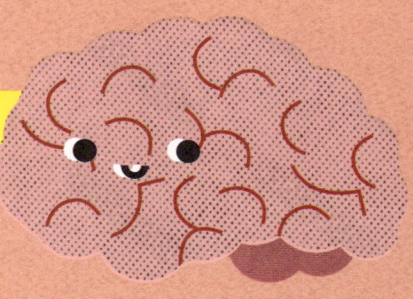

58

Identical twins don't have the same fingerprints.

Your brain creates about 50,000 thoughts a day. That's a lot of thinking!

The human body is made up of roughly 60% water.

Tears help you relax. Crying flushes out stress, so you feel better afterwards!

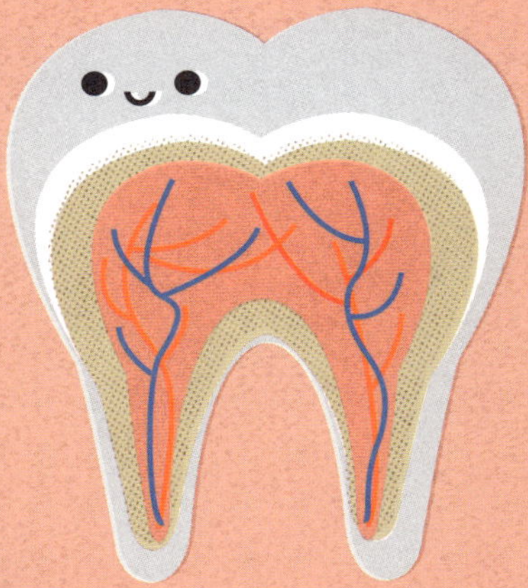

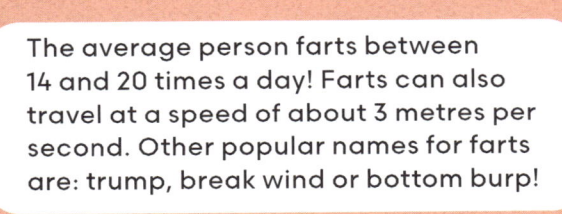

The average person farts between 14 and 20 times a day! Farts can also travel at a speed of about 3 metres per second. Other popular names for farts are: trump, break wind or bottom burp!

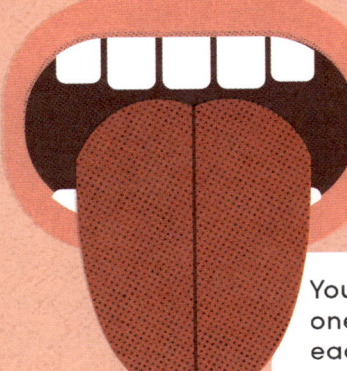

Your mouth produces between one and two litres of saliva each day!

The average person has about 1.6 trillion skin cells.

A newborn baby has more than 300 bones. Some merge together as we grow older.

Yawning isn't a sign of being sleepy or bored – it's a reflex your brain uses to wake you up and help you stay alert!

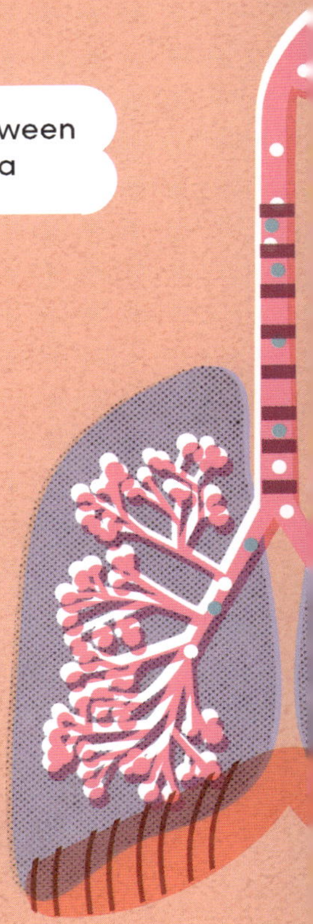

Glossary

B

Bacteria: Tiny living things that can make you ill or keep you healthy by digesting food and fighting germs.

Blood sugar: The amount of sugar in your blood, giving you energy.

Bone marrow: The soft inside of bones that makes blood cells.

Brainstem: The part of the brain that controls breathing and our heartbeat.

C

Carbon dioxide: A waste gas you breathe out after your body uses oxygen.

Carpals: The eight small bones in your wrist.

Clavicle: Also called the collarbone, this connects your arm to the rest of your body.

Collagen: A substance in your skin and bones that keeps them strong and flexible.

D

Dexterous: Having skill and control when using your hands, especially for small or quick movements.

Digestive system: The parts of your body that work together to help break down food.

DNA: The instructions inside your body that make you who you are.

E

Ethnicities: Groups of people who share similar backgrounds, like culture and language or where their ancestors came from.

Enzymes: Tiny proteins that speed up body processes like breaking down food.

F

Fibula: The smaller bone next to the tibia in your lower leg.

G

Genetics: The study of how traits like eye colour are passed from parents to children.

H

Hormones: Chemicals in your body that control growth and feelings.

Humerus: The bone in your upper arm.

I

Infections: Illnesses caused by bacteria or viruses entering your body.

Insulin: A hormone that helps control blood sugar levels.

K

Keratin: A strong protein in your hair, nails and skin.

M

Metacarpals: Also known as the 'palm bones', these are the five bones in the middle of the hand that connect the wrist to the fingers.

Metatarsals: The long bones in your foot.

Microscope: An instrument that magnifies tiny objects so they appear larger.

Minerals: Substances from food that help keep your body healthy.

N

Nerves: Thin, thread-like structures that carry electrical signals between your brain, spinal cord and body.

Nutrients: The good things in food that help your body grow and stay healthy.

O

Ossicles: Also called the ear bones, these three tiny bones in your ear transmit sound vibrations to help you hear.

Oxygen: A gas you breathe in to stay alive.

P

Patella: Also called the kneecap, this protects your knee joint.

Pelvis: The hip bone.

Phalanges: The bones in your fingers and toes. Each finger and toe has three phalanges, except for the thumb and big toe, which have two.

Protein: A nutrient that helps build muscles and repair your body.

Puberty: The time in life when a child becomes sexually mature, usually between the ages of 10 and 12.

R

Radius: One of the two bones in your forearm, on the thumb side.

Respiratory system: The parts of your body that help you breathe.

Ribcage: Made of 12 pairs of ribs, these bones protect your heart and lungs and help with breathing.

S

Scapula: Also called the shoulder blade, this bone helps with arm movement.

Sensations: Messages from your skin that help you feel things like heat, cold, pain or pressure.

Skull: The bones of the head that protect your brain.

Sound waves: Vibrations that travel through the air and allow you to hear.

Spinal cord: A tube-shaped bundle of nerves that runs from the brain to the lower back.

Spine: Made up of individual vertebrae, this column of bones supports your body and protects your spinal cord.

Sternum: Also called the breastbone, this connects the ribs at the front and helps protect your heart and lungs.

Synapses: Tiny gaps between nerves where messages pass through.

Synovial: A special kind of joint in the body that moves easily because it contains fluid. It helps parts like knees, elbows and fingers move smoothly.

T

Tarsals: The bones in your foot.

Tibia: The shinbone found in your legs.

Toxins: Harmful substances that can make you sick.

U

Ulna: One of the two bones in your forearm, on the little finger side.

Umbilical cord: The cord that connects a baby to its mother during pregnancy.

Further Reading

Very Well Mind
www.verywellmind.com

Brain Made Simple
www.brainmadesimple.com

National Geographic Kids
www.natgeokids.com

Science Kids
www.sciencekids.co.nz

Human Body Learning
www.humanbodylearning.com

Kids Health
www.kidshealth.org

Science Sparks
www.science-sparks.com

Britannica Kids
www.kids.britannica.com

References

Gray's Anatomy: The Anatomical Basis of Clinical Practice

Standring, S. (Ed.). (2020). *Gray's Anatomy: The Anatomical Basis of Clinical Practice* (42nd ed.). Elsevier.

Netter's Atlas of Human Anatomy

Netter, F. H. (2022). *Netter's Atlas of Human Anatomy* (8th ed.). Elsevier.

Look Inside Your Body

Stowell, L. (2012). *Look Inside Your Body.* Usborne Publishing.

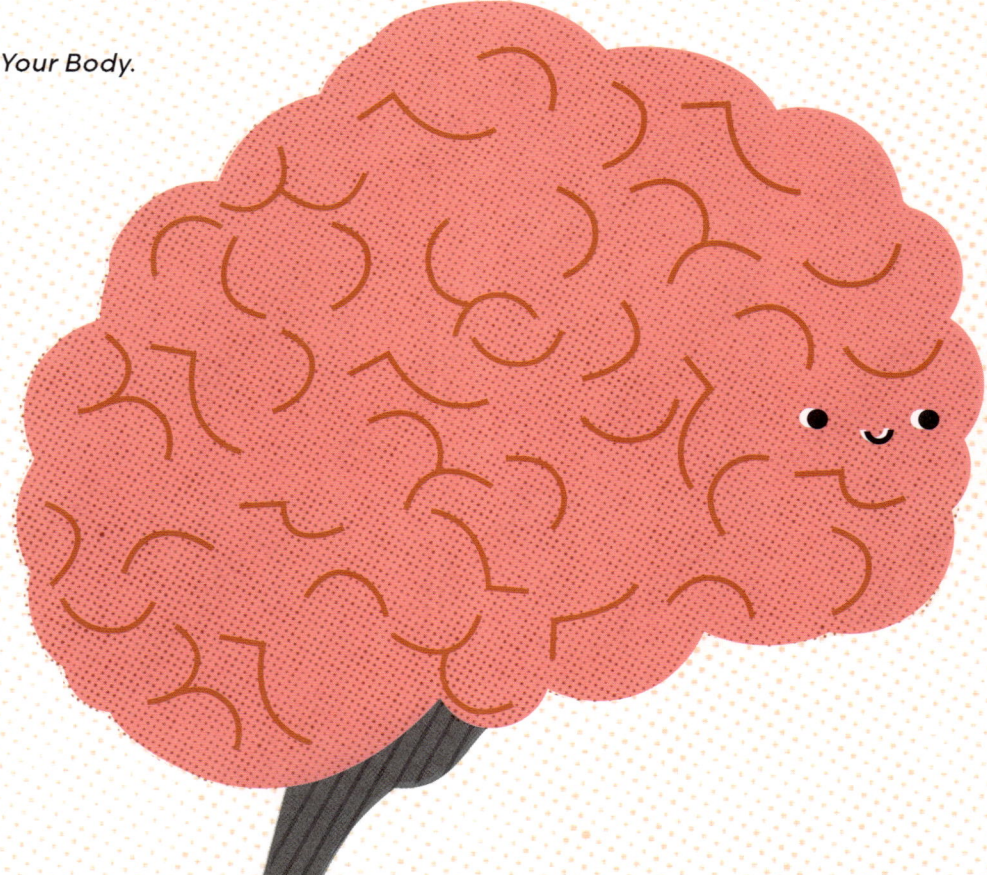

Human Body (DK Knowledge Encyclopedia)

DK. (2018). *Knowledge Encyclopedia Human Body!.* DK Publishing.

The How and Wow of the Human Body

Raz, G., & Thomas, M. (2021). *The How and Wow of the Human Body.* Houghton Mifflin Harcourt.

About the Author

Pui Lee (Scout Editions) is a designer and illustrator based in London, UK. She loves print, colour, folklore, drawing inspiration from everyday life, ephemera, travel, nature, vintage picture books, history and archives. Fun fact – she's also left-handed!

For Kyla, Mio, Kobi and Quinn
– my best art critics x

First published in the UK in 2025 by Post Wave Children's Books,
an imprint of Post Wave Publishing UK Ltd,
Runway East, 24-28 Bloomsbury Way, London, WC1A 2SN
www.postwavepublishing.com

A catalogue record of this book is available from the British Library.

All rights reserved, including the right of reproduction in whole
or in part in any form.

Text, illustration and design copyright © 2025 by Pui Lee
Fact-checking by Eryl Nash

10 9 8 7 6 5 4 3 2 1

Pui Lee has asserted their rights, under the Copyright,
Designs and Patents Act, 1988, to be identified as the author
and illustrator of this work.

ISBN 978-1-83627-023-2

This book was typeset in Scandia Line and Xanti Typewriter VF.
The illustrations were created and coloured digitally.

Printed and manufactured in China by Leo Paper Products in Heshan,
Guangdong, May, 2025.

This book conforms to General Product Safety Regulation (GPSR)
requirements.
EU authorised representative: Harriet Birkinshaw, Post Wave Berlin Studio
Email: GPSR@postwavepublishing.com
Address: Post Wave Berlin Studio, c/o Mindspace, Skalitzer Straße 104,
10997 Berlin, Germany

MIX
Paper | Supporting
responsible forestry
FSC® C020056

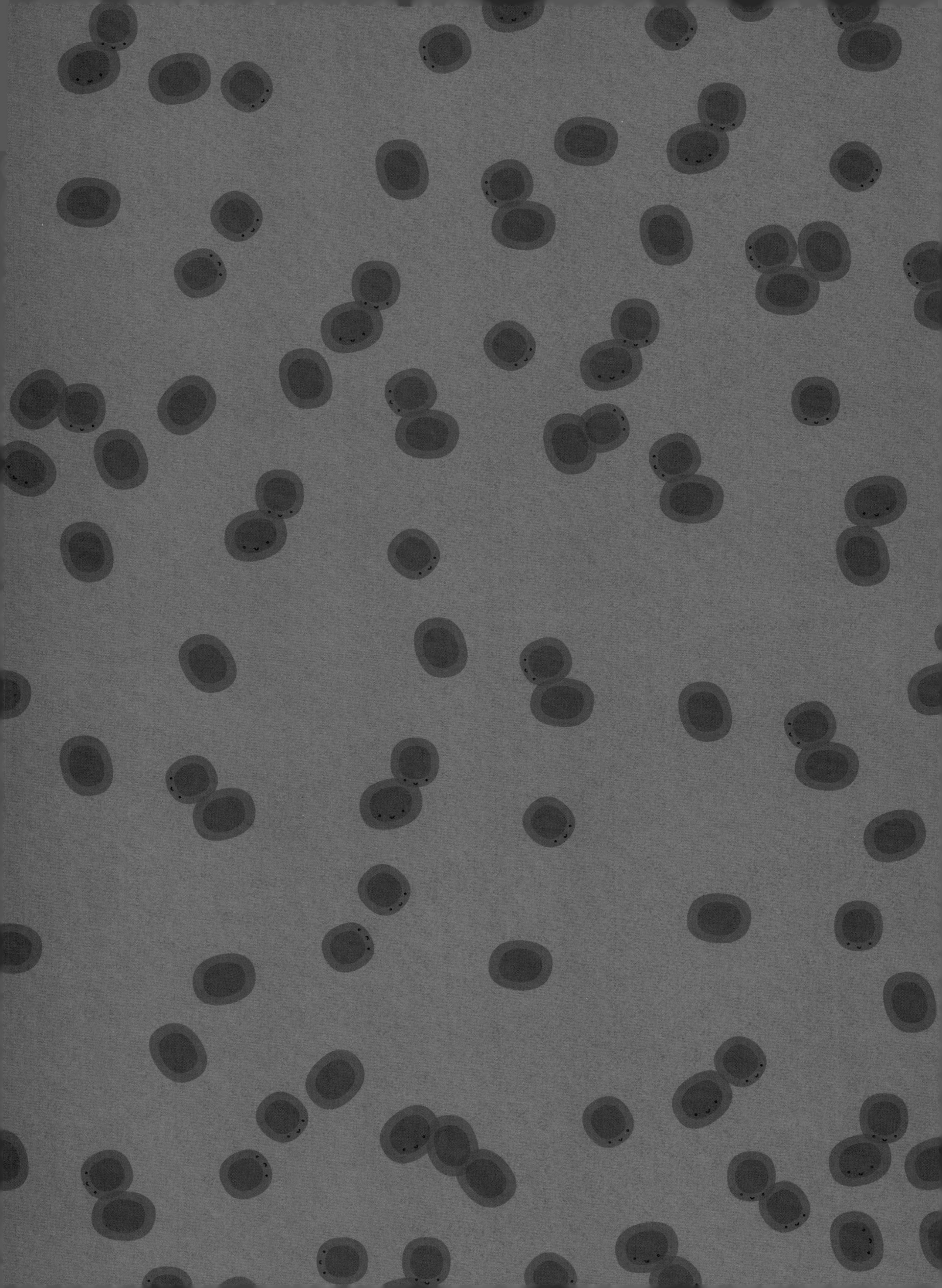

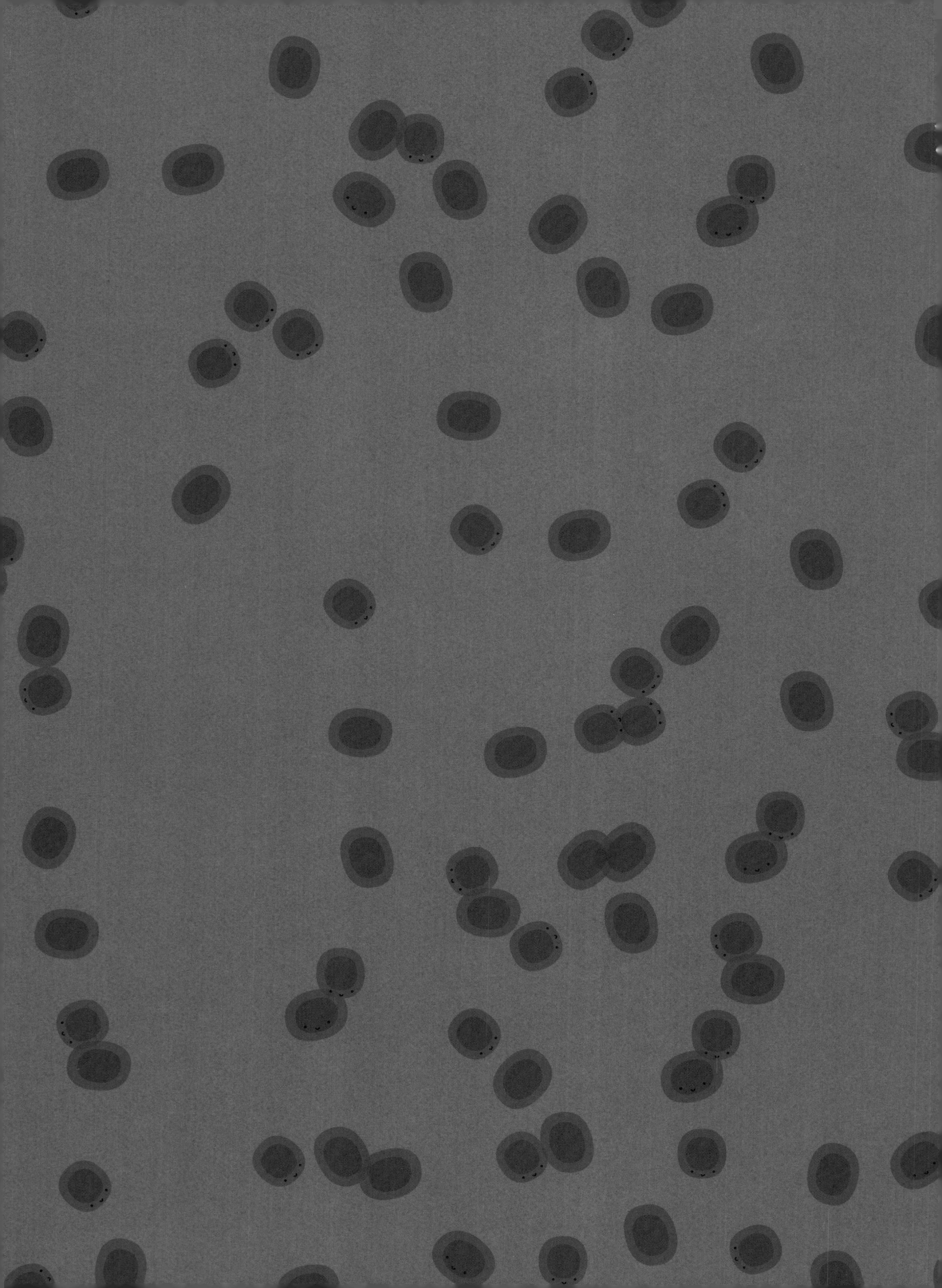